Uneven Pathways

Printed in the United States of America

First Edition

ISBN 978-0-578-13855-8

For the youth all over the world: In life obstacles occur but laying the proper foundation to capture success requires self-determination and genuine support from others...

Special thanks to Porsha Tay for the Cover Illustration: Being one of the many youth I formerly worked with and now being a mentor to you in your young adult years, I encourage you to utilize your talents in beneficial ways which will keep you on your successful path!!!

Contents

1. "It Was Written"

So... Today is the first day of school; yes I finally made it to the eighth grade in Junior High School! JaMir Wheeler is my name and I turned thirteen this month. Now here I am on this hot day - Tuesday August 24, 1993 and I'm getting ready for the first day of school at Washington-Howard Junior High. I'm looking forward to going back to school because over this past summer, I've gone through so many changes so I just want to be at a place where I can do great things and not worry about so much.

On Wednesday August 20, 1980 I was born at Queens Memorial Hospital in Jamaica Queens New York. When I was younger my maternal grandmother talked a lot about my mother and what she went through when she was pregnant with me. My mother's name is JayDa Wheeler; she grew up in Jamaica Queens New York and was raised by her mother which is my grandmother, Sharon Wheeler. My mother was my grandmother's only child and even though my grandmother was a single parent, both of them were very close to one another and my grandmother always told me how hard she worked to raise my mother back in the day. My mother was intelligent and loved to do hair; she dreamed of opening up her own Hair Salon after graduating from high school, following her completion of Cosmetology School. My grandmother was a Registered Nurse and had worked at the same hospital I was born in, until she retired in 1978. For some time, my grandmother wanted my mother to follow in her footsteps of becoming a nurse but of course my mother's passion was in the Cosmetology field.

During my mother's junior year of high school, she met a guy named Kenny Lewis. Kenny was a year older than my mother so at the time they met, he was a senior in high school. Kenny went to a different high school than my mother but they lived in the same city. Kenny was popular; he played on the varsity football and varsity basketball teams at his school and he had a part-time job on the weekends at a burger place, which was not too far from his house. My mother and Kenny met at one of the basketball games in which their schools played against one another. She went with a few of her friends and she noticed that during the time-outs, Kenny was staring at her. My mother didn't mind the staring because she had been staring at him as well; she thought that he was very attractive and talented. She whispered throughout most of the game to her friends about how she thought Kenny was nice looking. After the game was over and after my mother's team lost against Kenny's team that night, she and her friends hung around at the school for a while(it was something that many of the students and parents did following school sporting events). Kenny walked out of the boy's locker room and he spotted my mother as he was walking down the hallway by the gym. Kenny and my mother talked for a while, then they exchanged telephone numbers. My mother's friends joked about how she had a huge smile on her face during the ride home. My mother had her own car; she had gotten it a few months prior with the money she saved up from babysitting. She loved children and she would often babysit a few children in my grandmother's neighborhood. After my mother dropped her two friends off at home, she headed home and anticipated the phone call from Kenny.

Friday night my mother got home around 11:45 p.m. from the basketball game. My grandmother never went to sleep before my mother got home at night; she said she always waited up for my mother to make sure she made it home safely. As soon as my mother walked in the door that night, she ran over to the couch in the living room where my grandmother was sitting and had been watching television. She wanted to talk to my grandmother about the guy she met at the basketball game that night. Before she got a word in, my grandmother thanked her for making it home before her 1:00 a.m. curfew. My mother never missed curfew; she had it on school nights having to be home by 11:00 p.m. and on weekends or nights she didn't have to go to school the next day, in which she didn't have to be home until 1:00 a.m. That night, my mother talked to my grandmother about Kenny for a while and my grandmother listened to her and also gave her feedback. My mother's father left my grandmother before my mother was born, but his lack of help didn't stop my grandmother from taking care of her responsibility. My grandmother always talked to my mother about making the right choices in life and being careful with her selection in men. My mother told my grandmother how attractive Kenny was, about how talented he was in basketball, and that she heard he had a good job as well. My grandmother told her that she needed to take things slow with him by getting to know him. It was about 12:15 a.m. and even though my mother didn't hear from Kenny on the telephone that night, she was looking forward to him calling her before the weekend ended. Both Kenny and my mother had one another's phone numbers, my mother felt that it was only right for him to make the first call.

My mother watched the neighbor's young children that next day which was on a Saturday, and for a few months she would babysit consistently on every Saturday. She didn't have a cellular phone but she had her own phone and voicemail in her room. On that particular Saturday she went home after she had been working, watching the neighbor's children, so she planned to stay home for a while so she could wait on the phone call from Kenny. Around seven o'clock that Saturday evening the phone rang and she ran across her bedroom to answer it. On the other line was none other than the person she had been waiting on, Kenny Lewis. They talked on the phone for the first time that evening and ended up staying on the phone for three hours. The two of them both loved basketball and football as well as hip hop, rap, and R&B music. My mother was being raised by just her mother but Kenny was being raised by his mother and step-father. Kenny was the oldest of five children; his mother married his step-father when Kenny was just three years old and they had four children following Kenny. Just like my mother's father left when she was very young, Kenny's biological father left his mother when he was very young and she began to take care of him by herself. Kenny looked up to his step-father and called him "dad" just like his younger four siblings did. Kenny's mother was a school teacher at a local elementary school and his step-father worked at a construction company, which often involved some traveling. Kenny had a girlfriend but they broke up months before he and my mother met. My mother dated from time to time but hadn't had a steady boyfriend since the beginning of her sophomore year of high school. I'm sure my mother and Kenny didn't know where things would take them, but they started to get closer.

As weeks went by, my mother and Kenny began to get even closer and they spent much time together. After a week or two of talking daily on the phone, my grandmother talked to Kenny on the phone and my mother had also talked to Kenny's mother and step-father on the phone. When they went out on dates the dates consisted of going to the movies, out to eat, and when Kenny wasn't participating in his own sporting events they attended other sporting events together. Kenny had his own car just like my mother did, so they took turns driving when they would go out on dates; he often picked her up and she would sometimes pick him up.

They started to spend even more time together after their third month of dating. My grandmother invited Kenny over for meals and my mother also went to Kenny's house for dinners with him and his family. My mother and Kenny had talked about taking their relationship to another level and to be specific, they discussed the topic of "sex." My mother was a virgin but Kenny was not; he lost his virginity when he was fourteen. Both of them were very open and honest with each other during their relationship. My mother even talked to my grandmother about the sex topic relating with Kenny. My grandmother and mother talked about any and everything together, so when my grandmother was approached by my mother with the sex topic involving Kenny, she was more than willing to talk with her about it. My grandmother always told me that whatever decisions I made in life, to make sure I could live with my decisions. Just like my grandmother talked to me about making the right decisions, she always told my mother the same thing when she was growing up. Even though my mother died when I was a baby, my grandmother talked about her to me on a daily basis.

The summer before my mother's senior year of high school, she and Kenny seemed to be at such a great place in their relationship. The two of them took turns driving each other to school throughout the remainder of the school year, often picked one another up from each other's houses to attend church with their families, and even went to the beach at the end of the school year.

During the summer that particular year, my mother continued to babysit but she also took on a part-time summer job at a Daycare Center. Kenny had just graduated from high school at the beginning of June and had planned on going to North Carolina for college in August. Kenny really enjoyed playing basketball and football, but he got a full basketball scholarship to attend a school in North Carolina and he was so excited. My grandmother liked Kenny, Kenny's family liked my mother, and everything was going so well with their relationship. Kenny had extended family on his mother's side that lived in North Carolina not too far from the college he was going to attend, so he was comfortable with going down south for four years to attend school. My mother was so in love with Kenny that she didn't want him to go out of state, but she knew he was going to do great things with basketball and his education, by furthering them in college.

The summer had flown by and right before my mother and Kenny's eyes, it was time for him to head to North Carolina for school. My mother took the ten hour drive from New York to North Carolina with Kenny and his family, to drop him off at school. After dating for over a year, my mother and Kenny would be miles away from one another and that was a big change for the both of them. She was going into her senior year of high school and was planning on going to Cosmetology School following graduation at the end of the school year. Her plans after Cosmetology School involved her opening up her own Salon sometime in the future. Kenny promised my mother that he was going to remain faithful to her and that he wanted to marry her when both of them finished school. Kenny's family had gotten a hotel suite in North Carolina for the weekend so they could see him and spend the weekend with him before he began his first day of football practice on that upcoming Monday. My mother packed clothes for the weekend since she was going to be in North Carolina from Friday until Sunday. She called my grandmother throughout the entire weekend, letting her know she was doing well and what she was doing throughout the course of that weekend. Kenny's four younger siblings were good children and my mother enjoyed being around them. She didn't have siblings so it was good for her to experience some children who were like younger siblings to her. Most of the weekend Kenny had orientations and meetings so they didn't see him the entire weekend but Kenny's parents, siblings, and my mother visited their family which lived in North Carolina on most of that Saturday. My mother was emotional when she had to leave North Carolina on that Sunday to go back to New York because she was leaving the young man she deeply fell in love with. Kenny got a little emotional too because he had to say goodbye to his family and my mother, which was the woman he wanted to marry. Kenny got acquainted with his roommate who grew up in North Carolina and was also on a full basketball scholarship. The two of them were going to participate in some of the freshman festivities that were being held on campus, getting their books, acquainted with their class schedules and the buildings in which they were located, and so much more.

Senior year of high school started for my mother and even though she was excited, she was still a little sad because her boyfriend was in another state. My grandmother was retired but she volunteered at a local Nursing Home, helping the patients who were in the home for a few hours a day throughout the week. She still continued to babysit her neighbor's children on Saturdays but was no longer working at the Daycare Center because she wanted to focus on school during the week. She wanted to focus on school during the school year and not put too much on herself. Most of my family (maternal and paternal) lived in New York but they didn't see each other that much because everyone just did their own thing. My grandmother's parent's had died as a result of a car accident when my grandmother was twenty so she really didn't spend much time with her family, but she had a group of friends who were retired nurses like herself; they volunteered together, went out around the town together, and took out of town trips every once in a while together as well. My mother talked to Kenny everyday either after school or at night, and they would also talk to one another in the mornings before she left for school. During this time of the year at Kenny's college, he was participating in early morning basketball workouts, in which the college's basketball coach required the team to do.

A few months had gone by and it was already a few days before Thanksgiving. My mother was so excited because Kenny would be home in Jamaica Queens for the Thanksgiving Holiday. My grandmother had always prepared a large meal and even though she didn't see her family that much, they all got together on major holidays such as Thanksgiving. Kenny was back home for a couple of days for the Thanksgiving Holiday of 1979 and him and my mother spent a lot of time together during that short time period. My mother was still enjoying her senior year of high school; she had been nominated and crowned Homecoming Queen, was a part of a few school clubs, and was on the Honor Roll. Kenny was struggling academically in college and was on the verge of being placed on academic probation. Before Kenny left home to go back to school in North Carolina, he told my mother something that he didn't tell anyone else that was close to him. Kenny had befriended a few guys who were upperclassmen at his school, which used and sold drugs. My mother tried to get an understanding from Kenny as to why he was deciding to go down that path of destruction. Kenny told my mother that those guys really made him feel like he belonged to something besides his immediate family and the other members of his former high school basketball team. Kenny let my mother know he really didn't like college but he knew he needed to make something great out of his life after high school.

Kenny was back in North Carolina at college and school started back for my mother; the Thanksgiving break was over. Weeks had gone by and things seemed strange to my mother. She was calling Kenny more than he was calling her and it seemed as if he really wasn't making the attempt to get in touch with her. Kenny was hardly in his dorm room and when they talked, he seemed like he was too busy to talk to her because he was rushing to get off of the phone. Kenny's parents even began to worry about him; his mother called my mother one evening to talk to her about her concerns with what was going on with him. One night my mother continuously called his dorm room, but there was never an answer so she didn't talk to him that particular night. Kenny and his roommate grew to be good friends over the few months they had been freshman college roommates. The following day she called him first thing that morning in hopes of getting in touch with him, but there still wasn't an answer. After my mother hung the phone up from attempting to get in touch with Kenny, her phone rang and she immediately answered it. On the other end was Kenny's mother and she delivered some bad news to my mother. She let her know he was involved in an altercation and was in the county jail down in North Carolina.

One night Kenny, his roommate, and a few of the upperclassmen they hung out with, all went out for the night. One of the upperclassmen usually drove his SUV truck whenever the five of them went out and he indeed drove on that particular evening. They didn't know exactly where they wanted to go so they just drove around the town for a while, talking and laughing with one another. They all decided to smoke some marijuana which one of the upperclassmen purchased earlier in the day. Kenny's roommate received a call on his cell phone while they were riding and it was one of his female friends, so she invited him to a get together. He told Kenny and the other guys that were in the car about the get together and they all agreed to go ahead and head to the gathering. They finished smoking before they arrived at the destination, which was about twenty minutes away from their college campus. The get together was more like a party; the house was full of people everywhere on the inside and the outside. One question that Kenny asked his roommate was "Whose house is this, it's huge?" The house was located outside of the city in which they attended college and it was located on a large acre of land. There were no other houses located too close to that particular house, I guess it was the perfect place to throw a party! They all arrived at the get together which they saw as a party, around 10:30 p.m. Kenny and his four friends all entered the house together and seemed to be enjoying themselves. There was a lot of alcohol, marijuana, and loud music. Kenny's roommate grew up in North Carolina so he knew quite a few people who were there; he went to high school with some of the people that were there. Everyone that was in attendance appeared to be having a good time and there were many people who were under the age of twenty-one, which were drinking alcohol.

Around 12:00 a.m. the party was still going on and Kenny and his friends were still enjoying themselves. A group of guys walked in yelling with excitement and all had on similar outfits containing the same colors. It didn't take people long at all to figure out that the group of guys who had just walked in, were all in a gang. The guys walked around the party for a while then when they noticed Kenny's roommate, they approached him. Kenny saw that the conversation between his roommate which was going on between him and the group of guys, was getting intense so he gathered his three other friends, and they surrounded themselves around Kenny's roommate and the other guys he was arguing with.

Kenny didn't know at the time but his roommate was previously in a gang with those guys when he was in high school, but decided to stray away from them and the gang activity when he proceeded to college. Kenny got involved in the argument by telling the guys to leave his roommate alone and go about their business. One of the guys got into Kenny's face then Kenny pushed him, then they started to fight one another. Once he and Kenny began fighting, Kenny's roommate, three other friends, and the other guys that were with the guy in which Kenny was fighting, all were involved in a big fight with each other. People that were all throughout the house began to scatter and some people attempted to break up the fight, but it escalated to a level in which nobody could've expected.

The fight continued and many people started to evacuate. Out of nowhere, three loud sounds rang out from inside of the house and those sounds were that of gunshots. People started to look around to see what had happened and at that time, the fight had stopped. The guy that Kenny had been fighting was lying in the middle of the floor on the lower level of the house, covered in blood. He had blood coming from his chest and stomach, and he wasn't moving. Shockingly there was someone standing a few feet away from him with a gun raised. Everyone involved in the fight were no longer fighting at that point in time, and they were all at a standstill. Kenny was the one who was standing there with a gun in his hand and was also the one who had shot the guy he was fighting. Many people started to run but all of the guys that were involved in the fight were all still standing there with confused and shocked looks on their faces. The lady which threw the get together, screamed for a while and didn't know what to do. She had planned the get together and went through with her plans after her parents went out of town for the weekend.

The young lady immediately called the police, while still screaming and shaking from seeing a guy lying on her floor covered in blood. This young lady was still in high school and was a senior; her parents went out of town for the weekend leaving her home with two of her friends. When the police were in route to her house, surprisingly every single young man that was involved in the fight all remained at the scene which was inside of her home. Kenny stood over the guy he had shot for a little while then he willingly backed up and just stood on the wall that was behind him. Kenny's friends and the other guys they were fighting with all backed away from Kenny not knowing what to do or say. Kenny's roommate began to encourage him to put the gun down, while talking to him calmly. Kenny eventually put the gun down on the floor beside him then began to whisper to himself "What have I done," repeatedly. The police soon arrived and the young lady who threw the get together, began to cry hysterically while telling the officers that the commotion was downstairs. The police had their guns drawn as they had to for protocol, then they secured the gun that was near Kenny, then placed all of the guys that were involved in the fight in handcuffs. The police had to wait until the scene was safe before they could alert the firemen and paramedics that it was ok to enter the premises. The paramedics had worked on the young man and after a while of attempting to revive him, he was pronounced dead as a result of his gunshot wounds.

Many things were confusing to numerous people following the shooting and death of that young man. Kenny's friends wondered why he shot him but more importantly, they wanted to know where the gun came from. The young lady who threw the get together continued to worry about what would happen to her after her parents found out she threw a party at their home while they were out of town. Kenny's parents were confused about the situation, as well as my mother and grandmother. At the police station, investigations were done and everyone was released from jail that night except for Kenny. One of the worst nightmares ever had crept up on Kenny and that was the fact that he was in jail on a murder charge.

Kenny's parents communicated a lot with different attorneys following the day after he was placed in jail and charged with murder. My mother felt lost and cried a lot on a daily basis; she didn't understand what had went wrong with the man she fell in love with and looked forward to spending the rest of her life with. Kenny had been dismissed from the college he was attending due to the severity of the crime he was involved in. His parents planned to take a trip to North Carolina so they could gather all of his belongings as well as visit him. My mother had been feeling sick ever since the incident occurred; she expressed to my grandmother that she just didn't feel like herself. Kenny's parents had talked to him a few times over the phone when he called them from the county jail in North Carolina and my mother spoke to him on occasions, when she was at Kenny's parent's house. My mother was nervous when she went to visit him when she went with his parents but she also felt anxious because she hadn't seen him in a while. Kenny's parents and my mother only got to visit him for thirty minutes and during that time frame, the visit was done through a thick glass window, while the three of them took turns passing a telephone to one another to talk to him. Kenny was on the other side of the glass and he was wearing a dingy looking, one-piece, red jumpsuit. His parents talked to him first and then my mother stepped up and grabbed the phone to talk to him.

The visit was very emotional for Kenny's parents, my mother, and Kenny as well. Kenny assured them that he would be ok and that he had to pay for the horrible mistake he made a few weeks prior. The thing that made Kenny very emotional and difficult to stop crying wasn't the fact that he committed a crime, but it was the news my mother had delivered to him. My mother informed Kenny that she had been feeling sick and she felt so bad one particular day that she missed school, so my grandmother took her to the doctor's office. From that moment when my mother told Kenny that she was pregnant with me, he felt so disappointed because he let her down, let his family down, and more importantly, he let his unborn child down. My mother had already told my grandparents (Kenny's parents) the news on the day she went to their house before they left to go to North Carolina and my grandmother (my mother's mother) knew when they went to the doctor's office together. Kenny continuously apologized to my mother for letting her down and he told her that he didn't want to be the kind of man that wouldn't be present in their child's life. Before everyone knew it, the visitation time had come to an end. Kenny told his parents and my mother that he loved them and they told him that they loved him as well. Nobody knew what would be the outcome of Kenny's fate in regards with what Kenny's punishment would be when he went to court.

As days and months went by, Kenny still remained in county jail in North Carolina, and my mother was soon five months pregnant. She was soon looking forward to graduating high school. Things started taking a turn for the worst when she began experiencing some major stomach and back pain throughout the later months of her pregnancy while carrying me. My Grandmother Sharon became very stressed and worried about my mother's life, due to my mother having to often be hospitalized as a result of her stomach and back pain. The day came in early June in which my mother graduated from high school and even though she had been through so much dealing with stomach and back pain, she was physically able to participate in her high school graduation ceremony. Many of my family members on my Grandmother Sharon's side of the family attended her graduation and my paternal grandparents also attended the ceremony. My mother missed Kenny so much and they wrote to one another every week including five and six pages in one another's envelopes. She was due to have me in September and she was excited and looking forward to my arrival, but had endured even more difficulties.

My grandmother and mother went to one of my mother's scheduled doctor appointments not too long after she graduated from high school, and she got some very disappointing news. Along with me being inside of her, a tumor was found inside of her and was traveling back and forth from her stomach to her back. It seemed like things couldn't get worse for my mother; first she lost the love of her life to a murder charge and then she received devastating news involving her health. She was sent to a specialist so they could see what the next step would be and all of this took a toll on everyone who was close to my mother, including Kenny and his family. My mother had wonderful plans for her future following her graduation from high school which included Cosmetology School and a part-time job as well. Following the appointment with the specialist about the tumor which had been growing inside of her, things took a drastic turn for the worse.

Towards the middle of August my mother had to be rushed to the hospital after my grandmother found her on the bathroom floor in their house, unconscious. The paramedics were able to get a pulse from her and in doing so they realized that her water had broken. My grandmother was at a total state of shock and she feared for her daughter and grandson's lives. Doctors had no choice but to prepare for my birth; things had suddenly fallen apart but my grandmother was a praying woman so that's what she continued to do. The doctors prepped to perform a Cesarean Section to deliver me on Wednesday August 20, 1980. The procedure went underway and my Grandmother Sharon remained in the room with my mother throughout the entire procedure. I entered the world at approximately 3:00 p.m. on that Wednesday afternoon. After my birth, the doctors alerted my grandmother that the tumor which was in my mother's stomach and back, had traveled to her brain. At that moment my mother went into a coma and remained in a coma for a little while. My grandmother was a strong woman but expressed aloud that she felt so weak and helpless. She was at the hospital day in and day out at my mother's bedside and was in and out of the Neonatal Intensive Care Unit, where I was placed for a while due to the lack of oxygen I had lost before birth. My mother being a very strong willed woman both inside and out, fought for her life but things didn't improve with her health. Five days following my birth, my mother passed away.

On Monday August 25, 1980 my mother passed away from the result of the tumor that traveled from her stomach and back, to her brain. Following my mother's death, my Grandmother Sharon began to raise me from birth and maintained legal custody of me. My mother, father, and Grandmother Sharon often discussed different names for me and a decision was finally made. I was given the name JaMir Antonio Wheeler; my mother wanted me to have the same initials in which she had in her name and also wanted me to take after the same last name in which she and my grandmother had. My father wasn't able to make it to my mother's funeral because of his incarceration, but I know he loved her very much. My grandmother began to raise me from the day I entered this world. She always talked to me about how wonderful of a person my mother was.

A few months following my mother's passing, my father Kenny pleaded guilty to second degree murder; Kenny Lewis was sentenced to twenty years in prison. At that time my father was only nineteen so he would be around the age of thirty-nine when he would be looking at being released from prison. He was sent to a prison in South Carolina to serve his time for the crime he committed. As I got older and at an age when I could read and write, Kenny and I communicated to one another by mail. Along with mail communication, Kenny often called my grandmother's house to talk to me. I remember the first time I met my father in person was when I was five; I traveled to the South Carolina prison with my paternal grandparents and father's siblings who were also my aunts and uncles, to visit him. My Grandmother Sharon was very protective over me and didn't feel it was necessary or safe enough for me to travel from New York to South Carolina, until she finally decided to let me go when I was five years of age. My grandmother always sent my father pictures of me from the time I was a newborn, all throughout my youthful years of growing up.

Kenny's step-father luckily landed a big time construction job in South Carolina which was located in the same state where Kenny was incarcerated, so they decided to move to South Carolina. I was six when my father's parents and younger siblings moved to South Carolina. I remained in New York with my grandmother due to the fact she was my legal guardian. I went to church every Sunday with my grandmother and she was also the Lead Sunday School Teacher. I enjoyed attending church even though we stayed in church for long hours, Sunday after Sunday. I started being an usher at the Baptist Church we were members of, starting at the young age of eight. I was also baptized at the age of eight at our church by our pastor. My grandmother kept me in line and whenever I would even try to get out of line, she would either have a talk with me or enforce consequences on me. I rarely received physical punishment by my grandmother but I did get them a few times as I recall; she often told me "A hard head makes a soft behind." I began playing football and basketball at a young age just like my father did; Kenny enjoyed getting the pictures my grandmother often sent him of me playing in my sporting events. If I ever slacked off in school by getting negative behavior or attitude reports or if my grades fell below a "B" average, my grandmother wouldn't let me participate in my sporting events. We would attend the games and would sit in the bleachers or stands to watch. I couldn't be with my team and that would hurt me so

I rarely missed football and basketball games. I respected my grandmother and always told her she was my favorite person in the world, and her face would always light up with a big smile when I would tell her that. No matter what went on, we never missed church and we never missed any of my sporting events, including practices.

I was a car rider at school instead of riding the bus, so my grandmother would drop me off and pick me up from school on a daily basis. One afternoon at the end of the school day I was picked up by our church pastor. I was very concerned as to where my grandmother was and what happened because she rarely missed a day of picking me up from school. I was very close to my grandmother and didn't like it when things would sometimes change, even though change is a part of life. I asked my pastor as soon as I saw him, why didn't my grandmother pick me up from school that particular day. The pastor took his time explaining to me why my grandmother couldn't make it to pick me up from school. My grandmother had a meeting scheduled with our pastor at eleven o'clock that morning at the church, to discuss her will. My grandmother felt the need to get her will because she knew that she wouldn't be around forever so she had everything in writing regarding what would need to happen with me, her house, and other important matters if she were to pass away before I grew up and reached adulthood.

My grandmother always seemed to be a very healthy person; she took a lot of vitamins every morning when we sat together to eat breakfast. There were obviously some important matters that my grandmother kept from everyone and I found those things out when our pastor picked me up from school that day. My grandmother called the church a week prior to that particular day to discuss some important information with him. She always had short hair and for as long as I could remember, she had a close-cut hairstyle. I thought my grandmother just wanted her hair very short because she always brushed her hair before she brushed mine when I was younger then would say "Grandson I love how you look like your grandmother," she referred that comment to the fact that both of us had very short hair. When my mother was a teenager, my grandmother was diagnosed with Breast Cancer following her first visit to get her mammogram done. Cancer was detected in both of my grandmother's breasts and she went through chemotherapy. After she lost her hair she never wanted to grow it back, so she enjoyed her short haircut. My grandmother continued to get follow-ups about her cancer and for a long time, she was cancer free. Following one of her appointments when I was in the sixth grade, she was told by doctors that cancer had been detected in her body again. She was retired so she spent a lot of time volunteering and on other days, she would go to her weekly doctor appointments. She never told anyone she had cancer when she was younger and then when cancer was found in her body again some years later, she kept that to herself until she talked on the phone with the pastor one day to set up a meeting with him about her will. The cancer was rapidly spreading through her body and my grandmother was a small woman but was strong just like my mother was. Nobody knew that my grandmother was sick with Cancer until she told the pastor that particular day on the phone that she wouldn't have long to live. She had some wishes for the joy of her life, which was me. She let the pastor know that she would write everything down and give him a copy of her will, which had the specifics of who everything would be left to when she died.

The pastor had been waiting for my grandmother to show up at the meeting, which was scheduled at 11:00 a.m. Twenty minutes had gone by and the pastor was worried, so he called my grandmother but there was no answer from our house phone even after he called numerous times. An hour had gone by and the pastor was really starting to worry, so he decided to get in his car and go to our house to make sure nothing had went wrong with my grandmother. When the pastor arrived at our house, the front door was open and the glass screen door was closed and locked. He wondered why her car was home and why the door was open and he knew she was supposed to be at the church meeting at that time. The pastor went up to the door and when he knocked then looked inside to see that my grandmother was laying on the couch sleep, he started to call her name and pull on the screen door. The screen door was locked so he continued to pull on the handle harder, because my grandmother wasn't moving or responding to him calling her. The pastor continued to call her name getting louder each time then he yanked the screen door, and it came open. When the pastor finally got into the house, he immediately went to her and shook her so he could wake her up. My grandmother wasn't responding and after he noticed she didn't have a pulse, he attempted to revive her using CPR. The pastor couldn't get my grandmother to start breathing after attempting to do so for a while. In the meantime the pastor already called 911 and alerted them of what was taking place. When the paramedics arrived, they attempted to revive her but couldn't. My grandmother passed away on February 17, 1993 from cancer and to my understanding she went peacefully.

My grandmother was the only person besides her doctors, who knew she wouldn't be living too much longer.

Somewhere from the time she mentioned to the pastor that she had cancer for the second time and wanted to discuss important details with him to the time she peacefully passed away at home, she had been writing about the details of her life and her wishes for me (including the details of her will). My grandmother's house would be left to me when I reached adulthood. She carefully thought out and planned who she felt was responsible enough to be my legal guardian and that would be none other than the pastor and his wife. Even though we had family in New York, my grandmother wanted me to be with the pastor because they'd been friends for years, she wanted me to stay spiritually connected and grounded, and she didn't want too many of my structured routines such as school and my daily activities, to change or alter much. The finances of my grandmother which were left in her will would go to me, as well as the car that she owned but of course I couldn't get it until I was of the legal driving age with a driver's license. When the pastor finally explained things to me, I couldn't and didn't care about anything at that point in time. For some reason, I couldn't and didn't cry when I got the news that my grandmother had passed away from Cancer.

I knew how much my Grandmother Sharon loved and cared about me; we told each other that we loved one another on a daily basis. Every morning when she dropped me off at school, she would tell me she loved me and I would say "I Love You More Grandma," kiss her on her cheek, then get out of the car looking and waving at her until I no longer saw the car. I didn't think that on this particular day, it would be the last time I would see my grandmother alive. When she dropped me off at school on that Wednesday morning at 8:30 that was the last time I saw my grandmother alive. The pastor continued to talk to me and comfort me due to the difficult loss that I endured in my life on that day. What had to come next was the preparation for me to see my grandmother for the very last time, which was at her Home Going Service. So many people from the church family, to my maternal and paternal families, to my school family, and even my neighbors all showed me so much love by checking on me and being there for me during my time of loss. Less than a week later, my grandmother was laid to rest and on that day I finally poured out so many tears; seeing my grandmother's beautiful face that last time just really took a toll on me. From that point on, I began to write down my feelings and events that took place in my life in a notebook.

At the age of twelve I no longer lived with the most important person in my life. I lost my mother when I was a newborn, my father was incarcerated before I was born and had to serve prison time throughout my growing process, and now I had lost my grandmother when I was a pre-teenager. I was now being raised by the pastor of my church and his wife. Pastor and First Lady Brown had children but they were grown and in homes of their own, living their own lives.

My school situation didn't change and I remained at the same church of course because I was residing with my pastor. I was still a car rider but was no longer living in the house I grew up in since I was a baby with my grandmother. I felt welcomed, loved, and genuinely cared for by Pastor and First Lady Brown; they did a wonderful job of keeping me grounded, spiritually fed, in school, and active with sports. Now it was time for me to head into the summer before my ninth grade year of junior high school. Every Sunday after church, my grandmother and I would visit the cemetery where my mother was buried to put flowers on her grave plot and reminisce about her. I continued to visit the cemetery where my mother was buried and at that point in time, I began to visit my mother and grandmother's grave plots; they were buried beside one another.

My father and I kept communication open by writing each other. I also communicated with my grandparents and aunts and uncles; I talked to them on the phone every week, sometimes two and three times per week. I went to South Carolina the first week of my summer vacation following the end of my seventh grade year of junior high school, to spend time with my paternal family. I visited my father twice within that week and I enjoyed the visits; I could see that I took after my father's tall and skinny body build, and I took after my mother's light skin complexion and hazel colored eyes.

I really enjoyed the time that I spent down in South Carolina with my grandparents, aunts, and uncles, but I was ready to go back to New York for the remainder of the summer to attend some Sport's Camps. I was willing and ready to work on my favorite hobbies which involved basketball and football, so that involved me attending camps.

Pastor and First Lady Brown picked me up from the airport on one particular Saturday afternoon, welcoming me back from my week away with my family down south. When I got back to Queens New York, I relaxed for the remainder of the weekend besides going to church then to the cemetery on Sunday. On Monday morning I got up and prepared for my week-long visit to Chicago Illinois to attend a Basketball Camp. My summer vacation had been filled with different visits to various places including South Carolina to spend time with my paternal family, Chicago Illinois for a basketball camp, Knoxville Tennessee for football camp, Charlotte North Carolina for Youth Leadership Camp, and back to Queens New York for my last camp which was a week-long camp at my church for Spiritual Camp. Throughout my twelve almost thirteen years of life, I hadn't experienced a busy summer like the one I'd experienced that summer. The Browns had their grandchildren from time to time throughout the summer and I got along with them; they treated me like family and we called each other cousins. Time was winding down; it was coming close to the end of the summer and although my summer was filled with a lot of activity, I often felt alone because earlier in that year I lost my grandmother.

At one camp in particular, I met someone who had shared some of the same interests, struggles, and goals that I had. In Chicago I attended a basketball camp in which I flew to Chicago and stayed at a local Community College which was no longer open to the public for education, for a week. The camp was designed for youth ages twelve through sixteen, and we all camped out in a few of the older classrooms. They had different people come out daily throughout the week to teach us fundamentals, help us with organized games, and just incorporated basic basketball skills with all of the campers. While at the basketball camp I met a boy, Kemari who was from Brooklyn New York. Kemari was already thirteen, was going to the eighth grade in junior high school like myself, and had a twin sister who was one minute younger than him. Kemari and his sister were in foster care in Brooklyn and had been for a year or so at that time. Kemari and his sister's parents endured numerous struggles and after the Department of Social Services got involved, they were taken out of their home. He and his sister had three younger siblings who were placed with family members. Due to the lack of space that was in the home in which his younger siblings were in, their aunt and uncle were unable to take them. Kemari and his sister were placed in a group home until a foster care placement was available. Kemari and his twin sister Kamara had always shared a close bond and they wanted to be placed together, so after a short time of being apart in two separate group homes, a foster home finally became available for the both of them; both of them were so happy to be together again. Kamara was at a cheerleading competition in Chicago the same week we were at the basketball camp in Chicago. It felt like I already knew Kamara because Kemari talked about her so much during the seven days we were together at camp. Kemari and I became "buddies" during our stay at camp and we exchanged telephone numbers as well as addresses, when it was time for us to depart from camp and return to our homes in Queens and Brooklyn New York.

When I departed from Chicago Illinois and headed back to Queens New York, I immediately began jotting down notes and feelings which I often did on a daily basis. One important thing I started doing which I picked up from my grandmother was documenting my feelings on paper. I have a large box filled with notebooks in which my grandmother used to write in; she often told me "If you write things down, they'll never be forgotten." Kemari and I kept in contact and really became good friends. We weren't far from each other; Kemari was in Brooklyn and I was in Queens, which are two cities in the same state of New York. I was happy that I had a friend who shared a lot of common interests and goals as me.

First day of school went well; I sat in some boring classes, ate lunch, was picked up from school by First Lady Brown, then I went home to Pastor and First Lady Brown's house.

Something good that was happening in school and it was the fact that football would be beginning soon, and I was more than ready to play on my junior high school's football team.

In the meantime after some time had gone by in the beginning of the school year, I hadn't heard from Kemari in two weeks. I called Kemari's foster home where he had been living and asked for him and one of the foster parents told me that he no longer lived there. I was at a loss because here I was again at a point in my life where someone who I had gotten close to, left. At school one afternoon in my math class, one of the school administrators walked in the class and let the teacher know that she was getting a new student. The administrator brought a boy in the class and to my surprise the new student was Kemari, the boy I befriended at the basketball camp in Chicago and the same boy I had been calling and looking for. As soon as Kemari and I noticed one another, we walked up and gave each other some "dap." We had lunch after math so Kemari and I sat together and caught up on the events which had taken place in our lives during the two weeks we had lost contact.

On one morning while Kemari and his twin sister Kamara were getting ready for school, their Social Worker showed up at the foster home where they were placed. The Social Worker let them know that they would be moving to another home.

Kemari said that the foster home in which he and his sister were at in Brooklyn, was only temporary until they could be closer to their younger siblings. Their younger siblings were living with their aunt and uncle in Queens New York, the same city I was living in. Their aunt and uncle let their Social Worker know a few months back that they decided to get him and Kamara so they could be with their other siblings. Kemari and Kamara were excited to move to Queens New York to live with their aunt, uncle, and younger siblings. I talked to Kemari about the school's football team and let him know since the season had just started, he should play as well. Kemari thought it was a good idea and he wanted me to go with him to talk to the football coach, who also taught at the school. The coach was in the lunch room with us during lunch so we talked to him and he liked the idea of Kemari playing on the team, but emphasized the importance of him getting permission from his guardians and getting the required paperwork filled out.

Before we knew it, Kemari and I were playing alongside one another on the football field for our school. I was the team's starting quarterback and Kemari was one of the wide receivers. Kemari was my best friend, I talked to him about everything and we often spent weekends at each other's homes. It seemed like I was finally getting to smile a lot and look at the brighter side of things instead of focusing on the large losses I endured in my life. The Browns were doing a wonderful job of raising me and I always thanked them for everything they did for me. I got along with Kamara too; it was like she was the sister I never had and Kemari was the brother I never had. One thing that was certain at that point in my life was that the things I learned from my Grandmother Sharon, I would keep them with me and put the actions into play as much as possible. Writing things down which related with my feelings and never giving up on my hope and faith, was the ultimate goal in my life. At the age of thirteen "It Was Written" that I would keep striving for the best no matter what I was going through.

2. *"The Connection"*

Before I knew it the ninth grade which was the last year of junior high school, had approached and was already ending. During my years of junior high school which were seventh, eighth, and ninth grades, they had become the most devastating years of my life but had also become the most uplifting and eye opening years of my life as well. Life is very short and is filled with so many ups and downs, but there are times in which people or situations come along for various reasons, and that shows us that those connections fall into place for a reason.

Kemari and Kamara were two people who were embarking on a journey for success, just like I was. Kemari and Kamara were doing well in school, active on the school's football team and cheerleading team, and were doing so well with their living arrangements in their aunt and uncle's home. I continued to keep most of the events which were going on in my life written down simply to keep the tradition which my grandmother started, alive. Some people might think that writing a lot and keeping journals of my feelings and other events which were occurring in my life to be somewhat feminine, but I just do it because it helps me stay motivated. I didn't and don't keep diaries; I keep my deepest, hardest, best, and most loving situations written down so I'd never forget the things that occurred in my past. I often forgot to write something down daily but I would never go a week without documenting something.

Well, the time had come when the ninth grade had ended and it was already the summer before I was heading into high school. Kemari and I went to one basketball camp together which lasted one whole weekend but other than that, we just relaxed for the summer. Sometimes I spent the night at his house and sometimes he spent the night at Pastor and First Lady Brown's house with me. The Browns didn't adopt me and I didn't want them to; they just remained my foster parents. They sat down with me one day when I was thirteen and talked to me about what I wanted out of me living with them. I was honest with them and told them how grateful, comfortable, and loving I was to them for opening up their homes to me but I didn't want to go through unnecessary changes like legal adoption. Kemari and Kamara also went through a similar situation in which they didn't want to go through with the process of adoption; they were just comfortable with being in a good home at their aunt and uncle's house, and happy to be with their other siblings.

At the age of fifteen I often endured some difficult changes involving peer pressure, anger, and hurt. Although Kemari was my best friend, we had some times in which we physically got into altercations due to our major difference of opinions. One thing we always argued about was whenever we went to the local court to play basketball against other guys, if we'd lose we'd blame each other for the loss. So many things would happen at the court within that one or two hours we were there. Sometimes various men would walk up to Kemari and I while we were waiting to play next and would offer us drugs, other times we would see fist fights and would end up running home because we wouldn't want to get caught up in anything like that. One particular time I thought I wouldn't make it out of "the court" was when a dispute broke out while Kemari and I were involved in a three-on-three basketball game. Kemari, this girl named Monah, and I were all on the same team and were winning the game in which we were playing. All of a sudden halfway through the game, gunshots went off at "the court."

Everyone scattered in different places so I ran in one direction but didn't see Kemari when I finally made it clear out of the area of the courts where the gunshots were erupting from. I hid in one particular walkway which was on the way back to my house and waited there for a few minutes and then two people ran into the walkway where I was hiding. My mother, grandmother, and God must've really been guiding my steps and hearing me because those two people who had joined me in the walkway were Kemari and Monah. I hardly knew Monah and Kemari didn't know her either, but I was glad she was safe with us. We all waited in the walkway for a little while until we felt safe enough to start walking to one of our homes.

We finally felt comfortable enough to leave the walkway about fifteen minutes later. I always carried my basketball with me to the court but in the midst of running from the gunshots, I dropped my ball. That ball meant a lot to me because I got it from my Grandmother Sharon the Christmas before she passed away. That was one of the last Christmas gifts I received from her. In the midst of running, Monah picked up my basketball and when we began walking again, she gave it to me. While we were walking, Kemari and I got to know a little about Monah. Monah was visiting her older sister for the summer and she lived in Queens, not too far from Kemari's aunt and uncle's house. Monah was the youngest of three children; her older sister was twenty-five and had been married with no children for three years, and her brother was twenty and in the United States Marine Corps. Monah was fifteen like Kemari and I, and was also going to the tenth grade which was the first year of high school. She had been playing basketball since she was ten after she decided to stop dancing for a local dance company in Rochester New York. When Monah was a toddler, her parents noticed that she enjoyed dancing so they enrolled her in a local dance studio so she could dance. At the young age of four, Monah began learning tap, ballet, and other types of organized dancing. She participated in Dance Competitions with the Dance Company and continued to do so until she decided to get involved with recreational basketball, at the age of ten. She then went out for her junior high school's basketball team, made it, and played her eighth and ninth grade years. She always played basketball when she had free time and she was really good at it. Monah didn't like Rochester and really didn't like living with her parents because they were older and she said they were "old fashion." She loved being around her sister and this summer was the third summer in a row in which she visited and stayed with her sister and brother-in-law. Monah and her sister got along fairly well but they bumped heads when her sister would always get on her about her needing to respect their parents. Monah's mother didn't like the fact that she enjoyed playing basketball; she wanted her to stick with dancing. Monah's sister Mariah knew that their mother wanted something out of Monah that she didn't want for herself, but she always stressed the importance of her needing to respect others especially their parents. Monah and her mother had gotten into a big argument the day before she left to come to Queens for the summer. Monah's mother asked her a question pertaining to her not dressing like a girl and Monah told her she was an individual so she didn't like wearing dresses, skirts, or the color pink. Monah expressed to her mother that she should love her for who she is instead of distancing herself from her like she does and more importantly, she was hurt at the fact that her mother never attended her basketball games. Her father and sister always went to her games, but her mother would rather work extra hours on her job instead of going to Monah's basketball games. Her father was a retired police officer and her mother was a high school principal at a private school. Over that particular summer, her mother was offered a principal's position at a private school in New Jersey. Monah's father just went with the flow a lot of the time and would let her mother make all of the decisions. When her mother talked to him about the job offer, he didn't mind it at all and let her know he would be ready to pick up and leave.

Monah's father was the one who told Monah about the move, and she didn't want to move to New Jersey. By the time the new school year started, Kemari, Monah, Kamara, and I would all be starting the tenth grade. Monah and her parents would be moving to Trenton New Jersey. She talked to her father about finishing out the remainder years of grade school with her sister. Her father really didn't want her to move away from him and her mother but he knew she wasn't happy at home with them. Mr. Bailey which is her father, talked to Mrs. Bailey about Monah's decision regarding her living with their older daughter. Her mother was upset and felt as though Monah just wanted to do what she wanted to, so she went to talk to Monah. The conversation between Monah and her mother didn't start off well and for about fifteen minutes of the beginning of the conversation, they were mainly arguing at one another. Her father walked in while they were arguing and let both of them know how he didn't like the fact that their relationship wasn't good. Mr. Bailey explained to his wife that she needed to be more supportive of Monah, instead of pushing her away because she didn't want to be the way she liked her to be. Mr. Bailey then explained to Monah that she rebels a lot instead of expressing herself appropriately. He told both of them that he loved them dearly but he refused to let them tear each other down and apart because of their selfish ways. He told them that he was going to leave the room and let them talk to each other respectfully and for them to use calm voices, and to fully open up to one another regarding their feelings. In the meantime while Monah and her mother were having a heart-to-heart talk, her father called her sister Mariah and talked to her about her opinion regarding Monah living with her. Mariah let him know that she thought it was a great idea and Mr. Bailey told her if Monah's grades slipped once, she would be moving to New Jersey with them to be back home. Mariah had the clear understanding so he went back to let Mrs. Bailey and Monah know about the deal. Monah and her mother were having a nice talk when he walked in so he told them how happy he was that they were communicating calmly. He then told them of the plans to let Monah go and live with Mariah but let Monah know that she needed to keep her grades up as well as come home to New Jersey on holidays. Mrs. Bailey and Monah both liked the idea and it seemed like they were on a new path to build a better and healthier relationship between the two of them.

After Kemari and I got to know a little about Monah, both

of them came to hang out with me at Pastor and First Lady Brown's house. Pastor Brown wasn't home at the time but First Lady Brown was home cooking dinner. I went inside to get her and left Kemari and Monah on the front porch. I let Mrs. Brown know that I had a new friend that I'd like her to meet (she already knew Kemari of course), so she came outside to meet her. Mrs. Brown stayed on the porch with us for a little while talking and laughing then she offered Kemari and Monah to stay for dinner with us. Kemari called his aunt and uncle to ask them would it be alright if he had dinner with us, then Monah called her sister to ask her for permission to stay. Monah's sister spoke to Mrs. Brown on the phone and let her know that it was alright for her to stay. Pastor Brown came home and we soon all sat down to have dinner together. We all had great conversations and we got to know more about Monah. The Browns invited Monah to come and visit our church. Kemari had been to the church with his sister Kamara plenty of times.

While eating dinner, the phone rang and Mrs. Brown answered it. She talked to the person on the other end of the phone for a few seconds then she came to the table during dinner, telling Kemari he needed to go home because his sister had gotten hurt while practicing some cheerleading flips. I immediately asked Mr. and Mrs. Brown could I walk him home and Monah immediately said she would go with us. We didn't even care to finish up the delicious meal that was prepared for us; we were all worried about Kamara. Pastor Brown told me there was no need for Monah and I to walk Kemari home, he told us he would drop Kemari off at home and that Monah and I could ride with him. It didn't take us long to get to Kemari's house, he only lived about ten minutes in walking distance from the Brown's house. Monah's sister lived a few blocks away from Kemari and Kamara's aunt and uncle's house. Kamara was sitting in the living room at their aunt and uncle's house when we arrived with her leg propped up on some pillows. Pastor Brown walked in with us following Kemari and we were all concerned about Kamara. Kemari and Kamara were close so he was very worried and concerned about her. When Kemari got out of the car he immediately ran in the house to see how Kamara was doing. Kamara had been crying but was calm when we walked in and after Kemari asked her what happened, she explained to him that she was going into a flip and twisted her ankle. Her left ankle was swollen and red and she couldn't walk on it because it hurt her too much. Kamara's uncle said he was taking her to the hospital and her aunt was going to stay home with Kemari and Kamara's younger siblings. I considered Kemari and Kamara family so when they needed support, I wanted to be there and they did the same for me as well. I asked their uncle could I go to the hospital with them and he let me know that if it was ok with Pastor Brown, then it was ok with him. Pastor Brown let him know it was more than alright with him. Monah wanted to go as well so she called her sister and asked permission, her sister said it was alright. We went to the hospital with Kemari, Kamara, and their uncle and she was seen fairly fast. She broke her ankle and had to get a cast put on the next day.

Kemari's uncle Mr. Harper took Monah home then he dropped me off at home that night after we left the hospital. I realized that night that Kemari, Kamara, Monah, and I all had a connection with one another. All of us were in other homes with people who were raising us, instead of us being in homes with people who were our parents. We had all been through difficult times in our lives but were making strides to overcome pain and move towards the successful path in life. Out of the four of us I was the only one who wasn't being raised by family, but the Browns were very welcoming towards me so it didn't matter at all. The people who were taking care of us seemed to do it genuinely with so much open love and care. After the incident involving Kamara hurting her ankle, all four of us started to get closer with one another. Even though three of us shared one common hobby and talent which was basketball and one of us had a separate hobby which was cheering, we all started to be there for one another and support our individual talents. It took Kamara's ankle just about the remainder of the summer to heal but whenever we went somewhere she was right there with us. Kemari, Monah, and I joined a summer basketball league at the court in which we played different teams throughout the city of Queens; it consisted of three people who were teamed together. The tournament was an event which was organized every year for youth and adults, so that people could have something constructive to do. The tournament costs five dollars per week and the top six teams that won the most games by the end of each week would play one another then the last team standing, would win money. The youth teams were split up so that it would be fair and all adults ages eighteen and up, would play one another no matter the age range. Kamara had a specially made boot on her foot to support her ankle but that didn't stop her, she still went with us to the court down the street to watch us play in our basketball games.

Whenever we weren't playing in our games at the court, we were either playing basketball on my basketball goal at the Brown's house, going out to the movies or mall, or just simply relaxing over one another's houses. Kamara and Monah might not have had the same favorite hobby but they enjoyed hanging out and talking to one another about boys. Kamara and Monah had become best friends and of course Kemari and I were already best friends. We all lived in the same city which was Queens and we were all going to be attending the same high school. Our weekly basketball games were going alright; we were winning games but for four weeks straight, we didn't make it to the final tournament games involving the last four to six teams. Kemari, Monah, and I seemed to be working as a team but would fall short of winning within about four points or so. We started practicing more every day; it felt like we ate, slept, and lived basketball. The day before our week five tournament, Kamara was going to get her boot off of her foot and Monah wanted to go with her. Kemari and I chose to stay at my house and practice on our basketball because we knew we had to get our first tournament win; that week, we finally made it far enough to advance to the final round in the tournament. Later that day we all were so happy for Kamara because she got her boot off and the doctors let her know that her ankle had healed pretty well. Monah and Kamara came to my house when Kamara's aunt brought them back from the doctor, so Monah then practiced basketball with Kemari and I. Kamara sat in the shade painting her toes and watched us practice on our basketball skills. After we were finished practicing, Mrs. Brown brought out some fresh homemade lemonade. All four of us and Mrs. Brown sat in the backyard on the picnic table, drank our lemonade, and talked. I let Mrs. Brown know that I wanted her and Pastor Brown to come and watch us play in our tournament game that following day. The final rounds of the tournament were held on Saturdays and started at 1:00 p.m. Mrs. Brown let all of us know that she wouldn't miss our tournament games and she was pleased to hear we wanted her to attend. We all talked for a while then decided to relax for the remainder of the evening. Around seven in the evening Kemari and Kamara walked Monah home, and then they went home. We needed to rest so that we could be prepared to win all of our tournament games the next day.

That Saturday morning I got up early, showered, ate, and walked to Kemari's house like I did every day in the summer. Tournament Day was here and we felt confident about getting through to the first rounds, then making it to the final round. After everyone met up, we all went to my house because Pastor and First Lady Brown prayed for our safety and enjoyment before we left. The Browns were a family who prayed a lot and I didn't mind it because my grandmother prayed a lot. It felt like a huge family event because Monah, Kemari and Kamara's uncle, and Monah's sister all came to the Brown's house to join us in prayer, then everyone went to the court with us to watch us take part in our tournament games. Something about that day made me feel so comfortable; it had a lot to do with the support we had. Our first game started at 1:00 p.m. and we won that game. After our first game, we sat around watching other games until our next elimination game. Our second game which was one step closer to the championship game, started a few hours later due to other tournament games going on following our first game. We were on a roll, we defeated our opponents in the second round of the tournament. All we had left was one more game in round three, then the championship game which was the fourth game, followed. Monah and her sister Mariah, Kemari and Kamara's uncle, and Pastor and First Lady Brown, were all there throughout all of the games to root us on. The third game was very challenging but luckily we won by two points. After the third game which was the game before the championship game, we had an hour to go before we played in our final game. We had plenty of water, fruit, and little snacks in which Mrs. Brown prepared for us, to keep our energy up. Well the time had arrived for us to partake in the championship game and the seats at the court were crowded with spectators. The game stayed within a one to two point separation for most of the time; the other team would get ahead then we would, then we would fall behind in the score and they did the same. Through the one to two point leads and deficits, we triumphed in the end with a one point win over the opposing team. We won one big team trophy, three individual trophies, and a cash prize of three-hundred dollars. After the game was over Monah, Kemari, and I all thanked our families and care takers for supporting us. I told Monah and Kemari to come talk with me away from our people because I wanted to discuss something with them. I told them we should treat our people to dinner. Monah and Kemari didn't hesitate to agree with the plans and we were all so happy and appreciative for everything. We went back to the court and told our people the plans and they were all very happy and expressed to us that they were so proud of us.

We all went to the local Pizza Joint downtown and had a good time eating, talking, and laughing. During the middle of eating I asked for everyone's attention because I had to say something. I wasn't the type of guy to express many emotions, even on the basketball court I was never the type to jump up and down or scream if I made a shot or a nice play. On this particular occasion, I was overwhelmed with emotions. I began to express to my friends, the pastor and his wife, and everyone else about how grateful I was to have a support system like them. As I continued to talk, tears were rolling down my face and they were simply tears of joy, gratitude, and happiness. I then let Kemari know that I really valued his friendship and the brotherly relationship we shared. I told Kamara that she was a good person with a big heart, and I let Monah know how much I looked up to her as an independent female who enjoyed the game of basketball just as much as Kemari and I did. We all went to our own homes to relax after our dinner outing and we all had just one week left before school started. Monah, Kemari, Kamara, and I all would be going to the same high school. Kamara had already made the Varsity Cheerleading Team and had gone to some summer practices, as well as one cheerleading camp. Most of the time, Kamara had to sit and watch her team because she had the boot on her foot. A few months after school starts, Kemari, Monah, and I would all be going out for the school's Varsity Basketball Teams. Even though we were freshman and in the tenth grade, we wanted to play on the Varsity Teams instead of on the Junior Varsity Teams.

In the tenth grade things started to look bright and promising for me but I felt as though I was lacking the connection with God that I was taught to keep up, by my grandmother. It had been a few months since I had written anything down relating with my feelings, like I used to do. I was still attending church on Sundays and Wednesdays for Bible Study, and much of that was due to the fact that I was living with and being raised by a pastor and his wife. I prayed before every meal, thanked God for waking me up daily, and prayed every night before I went to bed. I wrote my father back every once in a while, even though he stayed consistent with writing me every week I just wrote him back when I felt like I had the time. I know my grandmother passed her writing skills down to me and it was a wonderful skill I inherited from her, but I just didn't seem to enjoy it so much like I used to. Something I held onto though was a necklace with a picture of my mother and grandmother engraved in it; I got the necklace made at the mall a week after my grandmother passed away. No matter what, I carried my mother and grandmother with me in spirit and even though I didn't remember my mother, she passed her strong will on to me which she got from my grandmother. Before school started back I went with my paternal grandparents to visit my father who was still incarcerated in South Carolina. The Browns put me on the airplane to travel from New York to South Carolina and then I was picked up from the airport by my grandparents. This was a quick trip, probably the fastest trip I've made to another state because I only went there for the day. I was fifteen so I was very capable of riding an airplane by myself. During this particular visit with my father, he told me how he messed his life up by getting involved with drugs and weapons. He really told me in detail how he took matters into his own hands when he shot another guy he had got into a physical altercation with, and the guy died as a result. My father let me know that he could've been on his way to playing basketball in the professional league or across seas but due to the decisions he made, he lost out on that opportunity. He also encouraged me to keep my faith in God, respect and appreciate the people who were taking care of me, stay on the right track in school, and to keep my athletic motivation. I felt comfortable with telling him about how at the time in my life, I felt alone. I explained to him that I lost him and my mother at birth, and that I really felt like giving up after my grandmother passed away. Even though I lost some important people in my life I had other important people who came in my life to help me, so I owed it to myself to make something positive out of the life I was living. My father only had five years left to serve out of his twenty year prison sentence; he'd been locked up since I was inside of my mother's stomach which was fifteen years at that point in time. After I left the prison, my grandparents took me out to lunch then back to the airport so I could catch the plane back to New York. I admired my grandfather for being a good man; he adopted my father at birth and stood by his son even though he made a big mistake.

During my last weekend before school started, I hung out

with my friends and enjoyed my time at home. A fact and conclusion that I came to was that I finally had a good connection with some people even though I had some disconnections that were made in my life over the years. The first week of high school was nice; I met some new people, enjoyed all of the pretty females, but didn't like the hard classes I had received. I took advanced placement courses and even though I didn't like having those classes, I knew they would help me prepare for college. If it was one thing that was certain about me, it was the fact that I was a hard worker and I wasn't a quitter. Before I knew it, basketball tryouts were approaching so I had to balance out my academics and basketball tryouts, which was all a five day ritual for a week's period of time. Kemari, Monah, and I all were going through the same thing and ultimately, we were all on an identical successful path in our lives.

That following week, all three of us got the great news that we had not only made the high school's basketball teams, but that we indeed made the Varsity Basketball Teams for our high school. Monah had made it to a goal in her life that she worked hard to get on, which was to continue elevating her basketball skills to higher heights. Kamara had gotten injured but didn't give up; she had continued to strive for her goal to remain dedicated to cheerleading. Kemari and I still kept our basketball skills intact and worked hard in every other area of our lives; our goal to do what it took to succeed was getting closer day by day. My father had walked the similar path in his life that I had walked in my life, but he fell off of his successful path, and honestly I didn't want to be like him at all. My Grandmother Sharon told me something only once which stuck with me and I would never forget it: "JaMir never try to be like anyone, your path in life is yours and yours only. Not even your family members or your best friend can lead you in the right direction, you have to lead yourself in the right direction all throughout your life!"

The school's basketball season was up and going and I knew I had to balance out my priorities by staying on the right track in everything I did. Monah was the starting point guard on the Girls' Varsity Team and Kemari and I both started on the Boys' Varsity Basketball Team for our first year in high school. Kamara's ankle had fully healed and she was doing well on the Varsity Cheerleading Squad. Along with doing well on the basketball and cheerleading teams at our school, all four of us were on the honor roll, doing well at home, and attending church every Sunday at Pastor Brown's church. Monah's parents traveled to all of her games and the fact that her mother was finally supporting her at her basketball games, made her happy and their relationship began to improve. Things didn't seem real to me: How did our girls' and boys' basketball teams both go on to win the State Championship as well as the Varsity Cheerleading Team winning numerous competitions, plus everything else was going well for Kemari, Monah, Kamara, and I at home, with our grades, and we were all attending church with the Browns every Sunday? I'm not perfect, never have been and I never will be perfect but I know that at that time in my life, I was happy and knew that I would be successful in years to come. I knew my mother and grandmother, who had both passed away, were proud of the man I was becoming!

No matter what went on in any of our lives, all four of us became the best of friends and made promises to each other to never let anyone or anything get us off track from succeeding in life. Even though we all adored sports specifically basketball and cheerleading, neither of us had goals of being in the NBA, WNBA, nor even be a cheerleader for a professional sport's team. During our many talks, we all realized that even though we had struggles in our lives, we needed to do something to impact the lives of others who went through similar struggles in which the four of us endured. I suggested to the other three that when we're willing, able, and of age that we should open up a Childcare Facility designed to care for underprivileged youth. Kemari, Monah, and Kamara all agreed with the plan I announced in regards with our ultimate goal, was to open this facility in the very city in which we all became the best of friends, Jamaica Queens. I would still continue to play basketball but my ultimate goal of devoting time, love, and care to younger people, was the first goal I was reaching for. I continued to pray on a daily basis and one promise I made to God, my grandmother, and my mother was that I would make the right choices and never get involved in situations that would prevent me from succeeding, such as jail or prison. I also made Kemari, Monah, and Kamara that promise and asked them could they all make the same promise and all of them did just that.

The communication between my father and I had gotten better by the time I was sixteen; we were talking on the phone at least two to three times a week and I didn't go a week without writing him, neither did I go a week without receiving a letter from him. At the age of sixteen I was a junior in high school, still played on the Varsity Basketball Team, and I had a part-time job working at the local recreational center tutoring elementary and junior high aged children. My strongest subject in school was math and I'm not sure how, but I understood the numerous methods and formulas which were involved in math. I found out by my father that my mother was good in math when she was in school. I realized that my father only had four years left to serve in prison, until he would be released as a free man. We talked about his plans following his release and his main plan was to spend time with the people who were most important to him. I had always told my father how close Kemari, Monah, and I were and he was pleased that we all had a tight bond. One thing my father emphasized to me was the importance of me staying committed to my positive endeavors and to never give in to negative temptation.

Towards the end of the school year of my junior year heading into my senior year of high school, the high school prom had approached. During a conversation which was held at school during lunch one day, Monah suggested that all four of us go to the school's prom together. When one of us had an idea, none of the others would disagree because we respected and loved one another as well as our opinions. We all put our heads together and planned on attending the prom together; Monah and Kemari were dates and Kamara and I were dates. We discussed the plans with our guardians and they thought it was a good idea. All four of us were hard workers and had part-time jobs, so we were very capable of paying for the things we needed including our prom wardrobes, tickets, and our meals. I was the one who was supposed to pay for Kamara's prom ticket, pay for our food, and pick her up as well as drop her back off at home. I didn't have too much to worry about because I had gotten my license when I turned sixteen and received my grandmother's car which was left to me a few years back. I drove my car and all four of us rode together. None of us were dating each other but we just planned on going to the prom as we did, as four best friends. Another great school year was ending, the summer was approaching, and my senior year of high school was just a few months away.

The summer of 1997, would be the last summer I would be in high school. Monah, Kamara, Kemari, and I all had full-time jobs during the week at a camp helping children who struggled with behavioral, emotional, educational, and some other difficulties they were dealing with in their lives. All four of us were leaders of our groups and we did different activities with our groups on a daily basis. The camp opened up at eight in the morning and ended at five in the evening. The camp was set up at a local school which of course was closed for the summer, but had cafeteria workers provide lunches for the campers every day. I was still a child myself but I was heading into adulthood so I wanted to be a leader by example for the children. Week by week the camp continued to go well and the sixty-something children who attended the camp, seemed to enjoy it. Some of the children resided with their parents, some of them were in the care of other family members, and others were in different placements such as group homes. Many of them showed up bright and early every day with smiles on their faces, ready to see what we had planned for them. Each week on Fridays we took field trips; the trips consisted of museums, theatres, the local amusement park, and other places. The summer was coming to an end; the camp went well, my home life was still good, my best friends and I were all in good places, and my last year of high school was finally starting.

3. "New Beginnings"

June 5, 1998 marked the day that I completed my high school education; I walked across the stage in front of my family, friends, and classmates and received my high school diploma. My senior year of high school seemed to be one of the best years of my life; I served as the Senior Class President, earned the Boys' Varsity Basketball Most Valuable

Player Award, was Homecoming King, I had received numerous scholarships to various College Universities, I was the Youth Leader at church, and the list went on. At the age of seventeen going on eighteen, I was a very blessed individual even though I had some major losses which occurred in my life.

My junior prom was wonderful as I attended it with my three best friends but my senior prom, I attended it with my girlfriend whom I had been dating. While working at the Summer Camp with the underprivileged children the previous summer for the first time during the end of my junior year of high school, I met this girl by the name of Tianna. Tianna lived in Queens as well but went to a different high school, and we were both rising seniors. Tianna had a younger brother which was in elementary, who had gone through some trauma when he was a toddler. When he was a toddler, he was being raised by his mother and she was a drug addict, so she ended up neglecting him a lot. Tianna and her brother had the same father but different mothers. A lot of things occurred in the home in which Tianna's brother resided in when he was a toddler, so his mother lost custody of him and he and Tianna's father was granted legal custody of him. Her parents had separated when she was younger and then her father had her brother when he met another woman, but Tianna's parents had reconciled their differences and had been together ever since. Tianna's brother was living with them and he presented some behavioral and emotional problems which stemmed from the difficulties that he went through in his younger childhood years. His mother went in and out of Drug Rehabilitation Centers and after a short time of being home from the last placement she attended, she got caught up in a drug deal and as a result, she was sent to jail then prison afterwards. Years later Tianna's brother's mother remained in prison. Tianna loved and adored her brother so much; that's one of the things that caught my attention about her.

After seeing Tianna drop off and pick up her brother Tre' to and from camp on occasions, I was curious as to who she was and how I could get to know her. When it comes to the children, I make that one of my priorities because it's my passion so I had to find the right time to talk to Tianna. It didn't take much time for me to meet Tianna; the second week of camp Tianna was the one to pick up Tre' from camp one afternoon during lunch, due to him having a doctor's appointment in which he had to leave camp early to attend.

Tre' had been helping me hang some pictures up on the wall one day at camp when Tianna walked in the room in which we were located. I thought she was one of the prettiest females I'd ever laid my eyes on and I certainly let her know that. We didn't chat too long because she had to get Tre' to the doctor but she took my phone number down and let me know she would call me.

I had a very busy summer that particular year and things just kept looking up in the right direction for me. Kemari and Monah were dating each other and had been for a few months; they really made a good couple. Kamara was also dating someone; he went to our school and was on the Varsity Football Team. Tianna and I went out on a few dates and after about a month or so, I asked her would she be my lady and she was so pleased that I had asked her that question. She let me know that she had been patiently waiting for me to ask about us being a couple. Tianna's family endured some financial issues for various reasons but they worked hard to keep their family intact. During the school year Tianna's parents wouldn't let her get a job due to their strong beliefs in her focusing solely on her education. Tianna wanted to help her parents with bills and often felt bad when they really had tough financial issues, but she kept her motivation in school and was a great role model to her ten year old brother Tre'. Tianna and I spent time together every weekend and from time to time, during the week. Due to it being the summer, she was able to work and now that she was done with high school, she could work as much as she wanted.

One evening during a conversation between Tianna and I while sitting on the porch at her house, she expressed to me that she thought about going to the Army. Tianna shocked me with that big piece of news because she was so intelligent and had been accepted to numerous colleges, but she was also a strong-willed individual and anything she set her mind to, she would follow through on it. Even though Tianna opened up to me about some shocking news, I had some shocking news for her and other important people in my life which I hadn't told yet. I had been looking into going to the military for a while but hadn't told anyone; I took my oath of commitment into the military that day. I decided to go into the military after getting a brochure at school and carefully reading up on the information regarding the military. I could've gone to college on an academic scholarship or I could've gone to college on a football or basketball scholarship, but I felt the need to serve my country. When Tianna told me about her plans to go to the Army, I was shocked but openly accepted it and she did just the same for me. The tough part for the both of us would be the fact that we had to tell our families and everyone else we were close to. I decided to take my three best friends, Pastor and First Lady Brown, Tianna's parents, her brother, and Tianna, all out to dinner. Tianna agreed that we'd both tell all of the people we were closest to, the news together. The money that was left for me following the deaths of my mother and grandmother, were still in my bank account and even though I just turned eighteen at that time, I had not touched the money. I had plans of donating a few thousand to Monah, Kemari, and Kamara so that they would continue with the plans of opening up the Children's Center we had planned on doing when we were younger. Along with donating money to open up the Center in Queens, I planned on providing money to Pastor and First Lady Brown so they could pay off the church's mortgage. Tianna was the only person I informed regarding those specific plans and she told me how proud she was of me. I also arranged to pay the total bill for the dining out expense at the restaurant that night. Everyone dressed so nicely that particular night and the outing was very nice. We all ate, talked to one another, and simply enjoyed our time with each other. When everyone finished eating I asked for their attention. I first let them know how blessed and thankful I was to have them all in my life. I started to get emotional at that point but even though tears were rolling down my face, I continued to openly express my gratitude. I first told everyone that I would be donating money to open up the Children's Center which Kemari, Kamara, Monah, and I planned to do years ago and I was going to name the center the "S & J Wheeler Children's Center." It was named after my grandmother and mother, honoring both of them. I then turned to my girlfriend Tianna and let her know how I was grateful to have a girlfriend like her in my life, and I prayed to God that He kept us together for a long time to come. I told her to share her news with everyone first and she did. Her family was very surprised but proud of her for her willingness to make her decision to go to the Army. Following Tianna's announcement I then gave my announcement. Everyone was surprised as well to hear that I decided to enter the service, in the upcoming fall season. Monah and Kamara immediately started to cry, expressing to me that they thought we all had the same ambition to open up and be the leaders of the "S & J Wheeler Center." At that very moment, Kemari stood up beside me and began to talk about how proud he was of me, and he totally understood that I wanted to go into the military. He put his arm around me and let me know that he, Monah, and Kamara would work hard to keep the center running well and help the children in the community the right way. The words that Kemari spoke really put me at ease and reminded me that I had some good people in my life. Monah and Kamara joined in and they let me know that they would keep our dream alive by working in partner at the "S & J Wheeler Center," doing what it took to help our children succeed. After I delivered that news, I then turned to Pastor and First Lady Brown and told them how grateful I was for them stepping up to raise me, following the death of my grandmother. I then took a check out of my wallet in the amount of sixteen thousand dollars in which I had addressed to them, so they could have their church paid off in full. The

Browns stood up and were at a loss for words; all they could do was hug me and cry. Soon Pastor Brown stood beside me and talked about how proud he was of me. First Lady Brown continued to cry but she talked about how proud she was of me and also emphasized how I was doing a great job of making my mother and grandmother proud. Last but not least I did something for Tianna's family and she didn't even expect it; I wanted to surprise them. I had a check in the amount of five thousand dollars to Tianna's parents; I knew they could use it. I was raised to give unto others and always be grateful for my many blessings, and grateful was certainly how I was feeling in my life.

While we were sitting at the table wrapping up our lovely time together, I was in the midst of a surprise myself. I had walked to the bathroom with Kemari to get myself together by cleaning my face, from the crying I had been doing. Indeed I needed to clean my face but it seemed as if Kemari was up to something, I just couldn't put my finger on what he was actually up to. He told me in the bathroom that God had so much more in store for me and he was blessed to be my best friend and brother. When I returned to the table low and behold, my paternal grandparents and my father were standing there. I was shocked and really couldn't move but Kemari helped me by pushing me in the direction in which my grandparents and father had been standing. I was embraced by my father with a huge hug; we hugged and shared tears together for a few minutes.

I was not only shocked to see my father out of prison about two years earlier than expected, but I was curious as to how he and my grandparents found out about the dinner that night. Tianna let me know that she talked to my grandparents a few days prior to our dinner gathering and had let them know that they should surprise me with their presence. When she talked to my grandparents on the phone, they let her know that my father would soon be released from prison. My father didn't want my grandparents to tell me that he would be getting released; he wanted it to be a surprise. Obviously my father did well staying out of trouble while serving his prison sentence so he was able to get released about nineteen months early. Tianna, my three friends, Tianna's family, and Pastor and First Lady Brown all left the restaurant at the same time that night. My grandparents, father, and I all stayed behind after everyone else left so we could enjoy one other's company.

Seeing my father in regular clothes rather than the prison uniforms he wore when I visited him, seemed strange. My grandparents let me know how proud they were of my father and I. My father was on the road to a successful life but due to a decision he made in his past, his successful path was altered and he had to suffer the consequences. My grandfather really didn't talk much but that particular night, he really opened up to my father and I. Even though my father spent time in prison and his plans in life took a detour, he served his punishment and was released from prison early. When it came time for my grandparents to express to me how proud they were of me, they both were very emotional and my father added to their words letting me know that I had been more of a man than he had been. I was very grateful to all of them for their positive words as well as their willingness to make it to dinner that night, for my going away announcement. My grandparents had also informed me that they decided to relocate back to New York because their other children were grown and living their own lives, so they wanted to enjoy their lives in the place in which they loved. My father still had things he had to do such as check in with his parole officer, be in the house at a certain time, and some other requirements that were put in place for him following his release from prison. One major requirement that my father had to abide by was that he had to reside in a halfway house; a halfway house is simply a home in which people live in to help them recover from situations in which they had struggled with and many people specifically adults, reside in halfway homes following drug and alcohol problems. My father's parole officer worked hard to get things approved for him to visit me in New York once he was released from prison, but he had to live in a different state which was in South Carolina. South Carolina was the state where he served his prison time so when he was released from prison, he was placed in a halfway home there. Usually when people are on parole or probation for major crimes they commit, they're not supposed to leave the state but my father's visit to Queens New York had been closely reviewed and approved. My father had to go back down south in two days so I wanted to spend as much time with him that I could because in the next month, I would be leaving to start out my career in the military. Even though I was eighteen and legally an adult, I still informed Pastor and First Lady Brown of my whereabouts, just like I did when I was under eighteen because I believed in respect and responsibility. At that time I had recently moved out of Pastor and First Lady Brown's home and moved into my grandmother's house in which she left for me. When I got home that night I let the Browns know that I would be staying at my grandparent's house for the remainder of the weekend, so I could spend some time with my father before he had to go back to South Carolina the next day which was on a Sunday.

I had less than a full twenty-four hour period of time to spend with my father but I wouldn't complain, I enjoyed the time I had with him. I got to my grandparent's house around nine-forty-five that Saturday night and everyone was in the living room talking, laughing, and having a wonderful time together. My aunts and uncles, who were younger than my father but older than me, were all over there with their children and we all just seemed to connect so well together. Somehow the topic of basketball came up and my father began to let me know how well of a basketball player he was when he was my age, and how he still had those same skills.

He went on to challenge me in a one on one game in my grandparent's backyard, on the basketball goal in which they had out there for the family. I emphasized to him that I was a better basketball player and athlete than he was and then I warned him to not break any bones due to him being "old" and still trying to play basketball. My family was all ready to see who would win in the one on one game between my father and I, so everyone including my grandparents headed out back to watch us play. Our game was planned to end with the victory score of eleven points; each made shot was worth one point, and the loser had to announce to the family that the winner was the better basketball player. Kenny Lewis announced to the Lewis family that I his son JaMir Wheeler was a better basketball player than he was. That night I had one of the best times of my life with my paternal family and I didn't want it to end. Reality had sunk in within me because the very next day, my father had to report back to South Carolina. Most of the family slept in the family room that night at my grandparent's house; we all talked and laughed all night and we didn't go to sleep until about 3:00 a.m. My father and I shared a wonderful bond that weekend he was in town and we opened up to one another a lot.

The time had come for my father to depart from Queens New York and head back to South Carolina. Most of the family accompanied my grandparents and father to the airport to send him off, including me. My grandmother was emotional along with a few other family members but I didn't cry neither was I sad. I wasn't around my father in my life so I didn't feel an emotional disconnection when he was leaving. I encouraged my father to get things right with his life and that I did indeed love him. He told me that he never stopped loving or thinking about me, and that he was very proud of me. After my father got on the airplane to go back to South Carolina, I went back to my grandparent's house to have Sunday dinner with the family. It was good that I was spending time with them because in the next couple of weeks, I would be heading to Texas for Basic Training.

My last two weeks in Queens, I spent a lot of time with Tianna, my three best friends, Pastor and First Lady Brown, and my family. I would soon be embarking on a new milestone in my life in which I was looking forward to, but I was sad to be leaving some very important people behind. At night I spent a lot of time writing letters to the important people in my life as well as writing personal information in my book like I did when my grandmother passed. I wouldn't have made it to the successful path I was on if God didn't bless me and if my grandmother didn't take care of me, so I had to write about them so I could keep my motivation and faith. Monah, Kemari, Kamara, and I got a head start on the beginning process of the Children's Center. I researched some options that I could go with to get the center open and since I had the funds to get the beginning process rolling, I had to think about the perfect location. I thought about the building in which we did the Summer Camp program; it wasn't used for much until organizations leased it for use but I had an even better idea. I would soon be leaving the state to go into the military for Basic Training and my house would be vacant, so I decided to turn my home into a Children's Center. I had to write out the proper plan and get the appropriate funding in place, so everything could be ready for the youth to attend the "S & J Wheeler Children's Center" in my home. A week before I was scheduled to leave for Texas myself and my three business partners who were also my best friends, all went to meet with an agency that assisted us with financial management in reference with the Childcare Center. All four of us were dressed in business attire, had our prepared documents, and were ready to start our business. Usually when a plan is designed, it takes a little time to hear back from people regarding approval but the company let us know how pleased they were to see young people such as ourselves, carrying out a positive ambition and sticking together for a good cause, so they let us know right then and there that we had what it took to get the process to the next level. I wrote the company a check to cover half of the funds for the youth for an entire year and they put up the other half of the money. We all signed documents and on that hot day in the beginning of September in 1998, we became the Founder and Co-Founders of "The S & J Wheeler Children's Center." I was certain that my three Co-Founders would uphold the center the right way and create positive impacts in the Queens New York area. Since the actual building was already present all we had to do was purchase the furniture and other needs for the program.

Word began to spread all around the city and throughout other areas of New York over the next few days regarding the opening of the Center, and it was producing some very positive publicity. I received a call from a local Furniture Company that wanted to donate some furniture to our center and we were so honored, grateful, and humble for the gift! Along with the furniture gift, we were blessed with the gift of a Painting Company coming out to paint the entire facility, were given brand new playground furniture, some computers, school supplies, and televisions as well. God certainly looked out for us by sending wonderful people out to volunteer their services and provide gifts to our program. Things were falling into place with the plans of opening the "S & J Wheeler Children's Center;" I know my mother and grandmother were smiling and very proud of all of our accomplishments. My next mission was to make sure the structure of the Center both inside and out, was approved by the city and state in order to complete the opening process. Monah, Kemari, Kamara, and I all got most of the work completed for the 'S & J Wheeler Children's Center" but the licensure and other inside work, Pastor and First Lady Brown let us know that they would handle that for us. I wanted the center to open before I left for Basic Training in Texas but it wasn't going to happen.

Spending time with Tianna was what I really enjoyed because we were compatible and through all of our personal struggles, we were dedicated to succeed and we also pushed one another to succeed. Tianna wasn't planning on leaving for her Basic Training until a week after me and even though she would be in Texas as well, I knew I wouldn't be able to see or talk to her or anyone else, due to the Military Guidelines. Tianna and I went to the movies, out to lunch and dinner, on walks, and just simply spent time with one another throughout the next few days before I left for Texas. While at the park feeding the ducks I said something to her that I thought I wouldn't say to a female until I was older and it wasn't "I Love You," it was "I Want to Make You My Wife!" I told her how she made me feel comfortable, loved, and important. I let Tianna know that I could see myself with her for the rest of my life, she was the only girl for me, and that I loved her more than she'd ever know. Tianna cried throughout most of our conversation but she let me know the reason she was crying was due to her happiness and love for me. That day was one of the best days in our relationship; even though we were going to be separated for a short period of time, the best was yet to come. That night I would keep our memories throughout the pages in my book and add to it as we grew together in due time. I dropped Tianna off at home then went home to pack for Texas; I was leaving in two days. I went to Pastor and First Lady Brown's house and opened up to them by letting them know how God put them in my life to keep me on track, and that's what my mother and grandmother wanted. I didn't remember my mother but they knew her and when my grandmother passed, they stepped up as parental figures to me when the one that stood in following the death of my mother passed away, passed away. All three of us talked for a long time that night and I was just glad to have extended family such as the Browns.

Leaving the place where I was born, raised, and had accomplished so much was making me sad but it also gave me a great sense of joy. Material things were nice and I enjoyed them just like anyone else would but I was taught by my grandmother at an early age that material things only brought temporary happiness. I would be leaving my car behind at the Brown's home due to me not being able to have transportation on base. I would leave many more material things behind that I definitely enjoyed but I was not going to dwell over them neither would I complain. The next phase in my journey of my life was there and I was so ready to embark on it. My packing was complete and my last day in Queens New York had crept up on me so fast; the next morning I would be leaving the city, state, and east coast portion of the United States for a few months. That last night I was in town before my morning departure, so many people came to the Brown's house to celebrate my accomplishment of going into the military. The get together was a surprise for me and so many people came out to show me love and support. I packed up the cards, letters, and notes I had received at my Going Away Get Together so I could read them on the flight to Texas, and I would look at them whenever I was thinking about home.

Well..... The time had arrived on that Monday morning in which I had to be at the airport in a few hours for my 9:20 a.m. flight to Fort Worth Texas. The flight was a few hours long which wasn't bad; at least it was one flight. I had some music to listen to plus I had plenty of cards, notes, and letters to read which were given to me by the many people back home! My flight was about four hours and I just used that time to reminisce on all of the times both good and bad, that I had back home in Queens. Within the first twenty minutes of the flight after departing, I began looking through my photo album of my mother which my Grandmother Sharon put together for me when I was a young child. My mother was a beautiful woman and I had photos of her dating back to her as a baby shortly after birth, all the way up to the time she was hospitalized for my birth. She wrote things down relating with her feelings just like my grandmother and I did; that was always a special interest and love that all three of us had in common. Included in my mother's photo album were a few written documents relating with her feelings, accomplishments, and other things. One of the last pages in the album was a letter from my mother addressed to her

"Unborn Child." The letter read:

My Unborn Child

As you enter this world that is surrounded with hurt, pain, disappointments, and negativity always remember to turn to the motivation into feelings that will leave you happy, proud, accomplished, and successful. Carrying you inside of me keeps you protected but as you exit my body and appear into the light of society, you have to grasp the process of life and all it has to offer. I love you my child and will forever love you, no matter if I'm physically with you or not. Keep God first, family second, and yourself at the forefront of your life!

Love Forever,

Mom

(Saturday July 5, 1980)

After I went through my mother's photo album including some of her writings, I then went through some letters I had of my grandmother in which she wrote a lot of. My grandmother often wrote letters of what was going on in her life and she would include Bible Scriptures at the end. Once I finished going through my mother and grandmother's albums, letters, and other written documents, I then went through all of the cards that I received at my Going Away Get Together from the previous night. There were cards from Tianna, Kemari, Monah, Kamara, Tianna's parents, Pastor and First Lady Brown, teachers, church members, my father, paternal grandparents, and other people in the community. I was very grateful to have so many supportive people in my life and I would never take them or any other blessing in my life, for granted.

I decided to listen to my music and rest for the last two hours of the flight. Even though at the young age of eighteen, I think I had an "old soul" when it came to music. I enjoyed listening to the great Gospel, Jazz, and R & B music from the seventies and eighties. I enjoyed listening to Rap Music from time to time as well but it wasn't as enjoyable as my other three genres. Shortly before arriving in Fort Worth Texas around 1:00 p.m., I turned my music off and made sure I had all of my belongings together so I wouldn't leave anything behind as well as saying a prayer to thank God for the safe travels. When the plane landed I started to feel nervous because I didn't know what to expect; for one I was halfway across the country in a totally different environment and two, I wasn't sure how I would adapt to the other people in the military. There were a few other people who were going to the same base in which I was going to on the plane, but we didn't converse until we got off of the plane.

Following the retrieval of our luggage from the inside of the airport at Baggage Claim, we spotted a gentleman dressed in military attire ahead of us holding a sign. The sign that the gentleman was holding read "Welcome new military recruits, Come with me!" Myself and the other four men who were alongside from the plane, all went and introduced ourselves to him. The gentleman's name was Private First Class Mitchell Jones. Mitchell had been in the Army for a little while and let us know how he made the choice to change his life after he was going down the wrong path, in his teenage years. During the twenty minute ride in the military van that PFC Mitchell Jones drove us in, we all talked and got acquainted with one another. Mitchell was just a few years older than us but he let us know that at our age we seemed to be much more mature than he was at that age. Before we knew it, we were pulling up on the base so we gathered all of our belongings and entered the military life. We were all taken to our stations in which we would sleep, we were given a complete tour of the base which was huge, and then we were given some time to unpack and set up our belongings in our stations. When we were finished everyone was allowed to call home to let our families know we made it safely to the base. The military personnel made it clear to us that we could only contact one household but if there wasn't an answer, we could try to contact an available person so they could spread the word of our safe arrival to the base. I spoke with First Lady Brown and she was excited to hear that I made it safely then she assured me that she would let everyone know that I made it safely. The last thing I told her was that I wouldn't be able to verbally communicate with anyone for a while unless it was an emergency so I would write them, then I told her I loved her and for her to give my love to everyone else. I often heard about Basic Training in the Military and I knew it would be hard work so I was physically prepared, I just wasn't sure if I was mentally prepared.

We were on a tight schedule with limited showers, preparation time in the mornings, and even with our eating at meal times. One thing I had to quickly learn was to not take my time but to pretty much move at a fast pace. Going to sleep early at night then waking up to do mile runs every morning during the week when it was still dark outside, really wore me out but it didn't take me too long to adjust to the schedule and routine. On Saturdays I still did some running but we didn't have to do the daily training in which we had to do during the week, on weekends. Saturdays were the days in which I sat back and read letters from family and friends, and I wrote letters back to them as well. I loved eating but I never had to eat my food in limited amounts of time until I went to Fort Worth so I had to get adjusted very quickly. I could never be too old to learn something and one main thing I learned from the time I entered the Military Basic Training, was to be very meticulous with my cleaning and organizing. I learned to make my bed a certain way that was required by the military which had to be done quickly, but very neatly. My military uniform regardless if it was the neatly pressed attire with boots and a cap or if it was the shorts and t-shirt running attire, all had to be neatly pressed with no marks, dirt, or other errors evident on them. The many others who were enrolled and committed in the Military Basic Training, I got to know them and started to build friendships with them. One guy in particular named Ian, had lost both of his parents when they died as a result of a hit and run car accident when he was just ten years old. The person who committed the hit and run accident was caught by the police two days later. The suspect was a twenty-one year old female who had too many drinks, so she obviously had been driving under the influence. The lady pleaded guilty to the charges and was sentenced to life in prison. Ian's parents had served in the military when they were younger and were respectable, productive, and well-known citizens in their community. Ian was in the fourth grade when his parents died and following their deaths, he started to get in a lot of trouble including him stealing, running away from his aunt's home (she began raising him following his parent's death), disrespecting his aunt and other authority, and other problems. When he was fourteen he was caught up in some negative involvement with some guys who were eighteen and nineteen. Ian sold drugs for the older guys he had been hanging out with, robbed people, and had even stopped going to school. Ian was placed in a Juvenile Detention Center (jail for children) for a few weeks then when he was released he decided to make some changes towards the positive path in life. He was hooked up with a male mentor who volunteered his time to leading him in the right direction. Ian went to a Military Academy High School from the time he was in the tenth grade all the way up until the time he graduated from high school, completing his high school education. Ian kept in touch with his mentor whom he called his big brother, and even when he entered Basic Training he was still in contact with his mentor/big brother. I shared some things with Ian about my past and how even though I had people around me that got into trouble, I decided to do the right thing. I was and still am far from perfect so I will make mistakes, but I promised myself that I wouldn't mess my future up and to that day I went into the military, I kept my promise!

I thought about the fact that I left home right before the Children's Center was set to open and I felt as if I abandoned my dream. Sometimes in life we set goals but somewhere along the way, we make a slight turn towards a different goal. Ultimately my goal of opening up a Children's Center had been achieved; I just wasn't physically in the center to assist my friends or help the children with their various needs. The center had opened shortly after I left for Basic Training and I didn't have to get confirmation that it was running properly because I had faith and trust in my best friends. Monah, Kemari, and Kamara were all in college in the city of Queens part-time and were also running the Children's Center. The center opened on a Monday during afterschool hours and on that Saturday prior, there was a Grand Opening Celebration at the "S & J Wheeler Children's Center." When I heard the news about the Grand Opening, I couldn't do anything but thank God and I shared that wonderful news with a few of my fellow military friends. I would be graduating from Basic Training in a little over two months and I was looking forward to that day when I would see my family, friends, and other supportive people.

Texas was so hot and even though I expected the heat to be higher than New York's heat in the summer, I didn't expect it to be that hot. The military personnel encouraged us to stay hydrated with water because weather as hot as it was in Fort Worth and all over Texas, could cause health issues such as heat strokes and exhaustion. I had asthma but I hadn't had an asthma attack since I had one when I was younger so whatever I had to do to not flare up my asthma, I would do just that. Being actively involved with sports such as basketball and football, contributed to me being physically fit in the military. The early morning mile runs kept me motivated and allowed me to gather my thoughts whether they were about my Grandmother Sharon, mother, or anyone else I had been thinking about in which I missed. Home was always on my mind and no matter where I was, I would always be thinking of them. So many chapters of my life had been opened, closed, and continued in September of

1998……. I was proud of the person I had grown to be!

4. "The Letters"

Saturday September 19, 1998

*Tianna hello my love, I know we haven't talked to or seen one another in some weeks and I really miss you! How is everything going at your Basic Training? I hope you're working hard but at the same time, taking care of yourself. I'm glad we get to write each other, we're both in Basic Training in the same city but at different bases so our personnel knows how hard we work and how busy we often get. Things are going well with me and I'm trying my best to remain physically fit. I love it! I'm going to write your parents before the weekend is over, I hope all is well them and Tre'. I'm so proud of Monah, Kemari, and Kamara for holding down our establishment as well as keeping our dream alive! I heard Tre' is doing well in afterschool at the Center and still being a big helper! Do you ever think about our future? I'm asking you*this *because I often think* *about you and I spending the rest of our lives with each other!*

I've met so many wonderful people here and even though we're all different, we're all sharing one common goal which is serving our country. I really enjoy it here and wherever this takes me in my future,

I'm sure it's going to be another blessing from above!

My encouragement to you is to keep your motivation towards the worthwhile things in life strong, for life is only temporary. Continue to do whatever it is that makes you happy and keep your support system close to you. Never let negative temptation get you off track. Well, I'm going to end this for now and get to the other mail I have to read plus respond to... I love you, take care and stay motivated!

Write back soon,

I Love You Very Much,

JaMir

(10:20 a.m.)

Our wonderful blessing JaMir,

How have things been in Texas? I'm so glad you're doing wonderful things in life, I know your grandmother and mother are smiling upon you! Brown and I are so proud of you and we talk about you all the time! It won't be long before we see you at your Basic Training Graduation, we wouldn't miss it for anything! The S & J Wheeler Children's Center is running properly, you'd be so proud of your friends! Brown and I still manage the finances there's nothing that you need to worry about, things are running so smoothly! We have been depositing your earnings into your bank account! Continue to stay focused and always keep God first, without Him your progression and success would not be present. I just wanted to send you a letter to let you know we love you, are always thinking of you, and we're so proud of you!

Love Pastor and First Lady Brown

September 16, 1998

September 19, 1998

Pastor and First Lady Brown,

Hello to the both of you, it was good getting your letter today knowing you were thinking of me! I truly thank God for the both of you, you've helped me so much in my life! You knew my grandmother long before I was born plus you knew my mother, so I know you two were the perfect people sent from God to take care of me following their deaths. I reflect on life so much and wonder how I'm still standing after all of the downfalls I've encountered, but I definitely knew that things happen to people for a purpose no matter when and if we fail to realize it. I haven't attended a church house but we have church service on Sundays and Wednesdays in the Dining Hall, and I really enjoy it. Please tell everyone I said hello at the church and give them all my love! You two along with other important people in my life, will be here to witness me complete Basic Training very soon and I'm so excited!

Well I'm going to wrap this up for now, take care and know that I love you both very much!

Love,

JaMir

(11:05 a.m.)

JaMir,

What's going on, how are things going in "Country Texas?" I hope you're settled in well, shoot you've only been gone for about a month.

Of course this letter is from Kemari, Monah, and I but I'm the one writing it (they're being lazy haha). We think about you so much and miss you more than you'll ever know! We saw Tianna the other day, have you communicated with her? She said she thought the military was the right thing for her but it wasn't. I hope you already knew this because if not, I didn't want you to be disappointed. The Children's Center is holding up so well including the finances, there's nothing you have to worry about. Kemari said that college is cool and he's enjoying it! Monah and her mother's relationship is unbelievable, it's like they're best friends! Me, I'm doing big things you already know how tough I am right? Don't waste your entire energy running and all of the other physical activity you have to do there, you know we all have to get a basketball game going when we come there in a few weeks!

Alright, hold it down and stay on top of your duties or you'll have to deal with us!

See you soon.....

We love you,

The Letters

Kamara, Monah, Kemari

September 16, 1998

Kamara, Monah, Kemari

What's up my wonderful friends, how are all of you? I was so excited to get a letter from you (even though Kamara was the one who wrote me haha)! I really appreciate all of you keeping our dream alive by running the Children's Center, even though I took another route! The three of you have been wonderful friends and family to me, I don't know what I'd do without you. I heard Tre' is still doing well and remains a helper, continue to keep him busy with positive things because he needs it! I wrote Tianna she was actually the first person I wrote but even though I was disappointed to hear she didn't go to the military, I did understand the fact that Tianna changed her mind because she's entitled to change her plans just like any and everyone else in this world! She finally wrote me a letter and I'll read it soon! So Kemari, you're enjoying the college life? Stay focused and have fun my brother! I can't wait to see you guys, I miss all three of you! I'll be praying for you and please do the same for me! Since I'm mailing this to you guys at the Center, make sure you tell all of the youngsters I said hello and I'm always thinking of them!

I Love All of You,

JaMir

(11:50 a.m.)

My Love JaMir,

Well first off how have you been? I hope you've been doing well! Me, I'm blessed and won't complain even when things aren't going well. I've been doing a lot of thinking since you left and I didn't feel as though the military was the right move for me. I've been close with my parents and little brother for years, ever since I can *remember. Going halfway across the United States just didn't set in with me and I thought I'd do well but after you left, I started to think long and hard about it. I'm enrolled in the local Community College taking up Nursing, I'm at a much better place now that I'm home closer to my family. A lot of my motivation comes from my family so I'm willing and able to stay happy while reaching my goals! Tre' asks about you all the time, he's doing so well you'd be so proud of him! I will be in attendance at your Basic Training Graduation, I won't be missing it JaMir!!!!! So, is the military difficult to adjust to? I'm sure you're doing well because you've always been a strong person both inside and out, and strength like that doesn't fade away!*

Don't worry about me, take care of yourself, you've always worried about everyone else so enjoy doing what you know is best for you!

I Love You JaMir,

Tianna

September 15, 1998

Chenelle M. Wiles

My wonderful Grandson,

Hi baby how are you doing? All of us are so proud of you, you should be proud of yourself! Those military people aren't working you too hard are they? You know how grandmothers are when it comes to their grands, I gotta make sure you're doing well! You've grown into a mature, productive, and loving young man and I can't tell you enough.. How proud I am of you! Your father talks about you all the time, he tells me that you are a better man than he's ever been. You're not only doing what it takes to help out this country but you're a business man and owner at the young age of eighteen! Never stop pushing forward, God has plans for you and as long as you walk the right path then you'll continue to prosper! Your grandfather is doing well, I can't keep him still most of the time but it's because he's always working hard, but is retired... Isn't that funny?

Hopefully your father can make it to your Basic Training Graduation, he's doing so well - I talk to him almost everyday. I'm proud of your father/my son, he made a mistake which caused him to lose out on a lot in his life but he's doing some great things and is simply blessed!

The Letters

Ok I'm going to let you go, I'm sure you have plenty to do. I'm praying for you, remember to pray for yourself!

Love Grandma and Grandpa Lewis

September 16, 1998

September 19, 1998

Grandma and Grandpa Lewis,

I've been reading and writing letters all morning and I'm loving it! It's good to hear from you and I really appreciate you taking out the time to write me. I'm proud of myself and I've come a long way in my short years of life. I used to think that my life wasn't worth living especially after my grandmother passed away but life is full of adventure, possibilities, success, and so much more. The fact that you stood by my father's side through it all, just shows how strong the both of you are. My father is a strong person too because he never gave up on himself!

I got a letter from him today and I will be writing him back soon. How are my aunts and uncles doing? I hope they're all doing well and taking care of their families! I really enjoyed bonding with my family when we had Sunday dinner at your house before I left town! You and grandpa are wonderful leaders of the Lewis family, continue to hold on to each other and keep the family close! I look forward to seeing you two soon, take care...

Love JaMir

(12:20 p.m.)

September 19, 1998

Tianna,

It was good getting a letter from you today, I've been

thinking about you! I'm doing well and have been adjusting well enough, it's really interesting being a part of the military. Tianna my girl, never feel bad about changing your career path especially if it's not harming you or anyone else. I'm proud of you for still doing great things in your life! I miss you so much, you're my girl and I hope we continue to grow together even though we're miles away from each other right now. Please tell Tre' I said hi and for him to continue doing well! How are your parents? I try to write so many people so I can keep in touch, sometimes I write so much in my personal journal that I often forget that I have people back home who need to get letters from me. I never go a day without thinking about all of you, I can't wait until I get to see and spend time with everyone! How's school going? I know your studies often get overwhelming but you're an intelligent person, stay motivated! We get to watch t.v. especially on weekends so I catch up on my sports and the latest news around the world.

Keep me posted on how things are going in Queens please. Write me back soon and I love you very much!

JaMir

(1:00 p.m.)

Son,

How's everything down there in Texas? I hope all is well, I'm so proud of you! Man you've become a wonderful, successful, and upstanding person! I know your mother and grandmother would be so proud of you, they're always watching you son you know that right! So, tell me what kind of things you do on base? Do you run and work out a lot? Do you play basketball at all? I have a job in construction down here in South Carolina, I really like my job! I'm still staying in the halfway house, I should be getting something stable within the next month or so. I'm trying to plan on coming with your grandparents to the graduation, I work all of the time though. Do you need anything? I'm at a place in my life where I can step up and help you financially, although it may not be a lot I still can help you son! I want to apologize for not being the man and father I should've been to you. I had a good life and was doing the right things but I started to do negative things. I know there are no excuses for the things I did. Not being there for your mother and not being there for you has really made me upset with myself so many times in my life, but I can't turn back the hands of time. If I could rewind all of my mistakes and do things the right way, there's no doubt about it.... I WOULD! I hope you can find it in your heart to forgive me, I've always told you that you're a better man than I've ever been and I mean that! Keep doing great things man and I love you more than life itself!

Love Pops

September 15, 1998

September 19, 1998

What's up Pops,

It was good hearing from you and to know you're doing well! I'm fine, no need to worry about me. Texas is really hot but I'm enjoying the military lifestyle. I keep my mother and grandmother's memories alive by staying on top of my positive endeavors and keeping my faith! I

Chenelle M. Wiles

I forgive you and I'm not mad or disappointed in you, everyone makes mistakes pop. What you need to do is continue to improve your life and make amends with the man's family in which you were involved in the altercation with, who died as a result. One thing we all have to do in life is learn how to get through our toughest times. I'd love to see you on one of the most important days of my life but you have to take care of yourself first, before you can attempt to make sure others are well. I love you and I'm proud of you for making improvements in your life! Take things one day and one step at a time in life, remember that life is very short so live it to the fullest!

I'll talk to you soon, write back "old man." Love you

Pop..

(1:45 p.m.)

September 15, 1998

Hi JaMir,

How are you doing? I miss you. You were always nice to me. I'm being good. I help out all the time at the Center. I'm glad my sister is home and didn't go to Texas because I would have missed her too much. She always talks about you and tells me that you are a good boyfriend. I hope she marries you because you are a good man. I talk to my therapist a lot now and we have good talks about my mom, school, and even about you. I'm making A's and B's in school and I think I might go out for the school basketball team. Thank you for always helping me and being nice to me. I hope you like it in the military, listen to those people just like you told me to listen to adults that help me.

See you later.

Love Tre'

Chenelle M. Wiles

September 19, 1998

My buddy Tre',

I was so happy to see I had a letter from you! I'm proud of you, I always knew you could do great things man so just continue to stay on the right path. I've been hearing some wonderful things about you, you've been a great helper at the Center.. THANK YOU! As you get older just take the steps to do the right things and never let anyone talk you into doing negative things. Whatever positive things you set your mind to, you will achieve them you just have to stay motivated! Thank you Tre' for thanking me and complimenting me, you're such a generous young man. Hopefully I'll see you soon, never stop pushing forward ok?

Love JaMir

(2:30 p.m.)

Hello JaMir,

We wanted to let you know how proud we are of you! The Youth Department misses you so much but we know God is protecting you as you're in Texas doing great things! Pastor and First Lady Brown send up prayers and blessings all the time and the congregation sends theirs up for you as well! Are you able to get involved in church on base? We know you're very busy doing various physical things while you're in Basic Training, never lose your faith JaMir. You're such an encouragement and blessing to so many people, God has really blessed you!

Alright stay safe and prayed up, we all love you JaMir!

Love the Youth Department

September 16, 1998

Well well well,

One of my favorite students of all time Mr. JaMir Wheeler, how are you? It's such a pleasure to witness how much you've grown mentally, emotionally, spiritually, and intellectually! Just a few months ago you were sitting in my English class excelling and being the wonderful leader you are! No matter what obstacles entered your path, you gave everything your all and that's why you're standing tall today! Are you still doing a lot of writing in your spare time? You were so talented with your writing skills! When do you graduate from Basic Training? Stay focused JaMir, it's really a pleasure for me to be a witness of how you've overcome so many obstacles and many more obstacles will creep up on you in life, so just knock them down and continue to succeed!!!

Write me back when you can, stay strong!

Mr. Mitchell

September 15, 1998

My wonderful Church Family/Youth Department,

What a joy it was to get a letter from you, I think about you all a lot! How are all of you? God is so good isn't He! I attend services on base every Sunday morning, I read my Bible, and am constantly praying! Thank you for keeping me in prayer! I really appreciate all of you! I'll be graduating from Basic Training in a little over a month, I've really embraced this opportunity in the military. I'll never stop thinking about how blessed I am so I will forever thank Him for all He has done, all He is doing, and all He will do! Let all of the youth know that I love them and for them to stay encouraged for the right reasons! Pastor and First Lady Brown are wonderful leaders of the church!

Much Love and Thanks to All of You,

JaMir

(3:00 p.m.) – September 19, 1998

Chenelle M. Wiles

September 19, 1998

What's been going on Mr. Mitchell, it was good hearing from you?!?! I really enjoyed high school, especially being in your class! If I could I would turn back the hands of time and go back to my childhood years but I wish my mother would've been alive as well as my grandmother. Remember when I wrote that poem titled "Mom and Grandma," I still have that!!!!! I appreciate you taking out the time to listen to me when I was in your class and I certainly appreciate you reaching out to communicate with me right now as well! Oh and you were definitely my favorite teacher, no doubt about it! No worries, I will stay focused because I won't accept anything less from myself.

Please keep in touch with me as I will do the same with you!
Thank you again for everything!

JaMir

(3:45 p.m.)

I spent much of my Saturday reading letters which were sent to me from important people back home and I responded to them as well. I had an even larger level of motivation following Sunday because I knew if people took the time to keep in touch with me, then I could continue to do what it took to succeed! I never thought about serving in the military when I was a young child, it was at the time in my life when I became an adult that I felt the need to serve my country. I could've been going to any Division One School to play basketball, living the life of a college basketball student, and studying something like Sports Medicine, but I preferred to go after a different goal. As I stuck with my alternative goal of going into the military, I knew that the other people I encouraged in my life could do whatever they wanted and would achieve, as long as they didn't get off of the right path.

Along with the letters in which I wrote back to Queens and the ones I received from my people back home in Queens, I knew I had to turn back the hands of time with my writing in relation with my feelings to God, my mother, and my Grandmother Sharon. I took many of the writings in which my grandmother used to document before she passed away, with me to Texas. I didn't have many but I had a few papers from the past when my mother was younger in which she wrote, with me on base as well. Even though I no longer have my mother and grandmother with me physically, I still carry the memories of the times I spent with my grandmother and the important material items I still have of them such as pictures, notes, and other important items, with me in my heart.

My father opened up to me about the regrets he had, the night we both stayed at his parents/my grandparent's house, before he had to go back to South Carolina. He told me that he regretted the decisions he made when he chose to get involved with drugs, hanging around the wrong people, and having the gun which led to the bad decision of him taking someone else's life. He told me something that night that I'd never forget and it was: "You can have all of the strength you think it takes to do certain things but the strongest skills come from within us!" I not only forgave my father for not being a part of my life but at that moment I accepted the fact that there were certain situations in my life that I could control, and there were other situations I couldn't control.

Sunday September 20, 1998 before I went to sleep, I went through some of the writings I had in my possession. I had my grandmother's notebook which she kept before she passed and it included many documents in which my mother wrote when she was a teenager, as well as her own documents she wrote. This was one of the letters I read that night:

Wednesday August 20, 1980

I sit here beside my daughter in the hospital, wondering why certain things in life occur, but even though I wonder

I also know that everything is God's purpose and will. My grandson JaMir entered this world today and I'm so grateful to God for him, what a lovely and blessed gift he is. In the midst of it all, my baby JayDa is very sick in this hospital bed beside me. Lord I ask you to heal her, I also ask you to look over my grandson – that he grows up to be a healthy, productive, God loving and serving, and successful individual in life. Through all of the pain, I acknowledge that you are the only one who makes anything possible, thank you for it all! Life is very short and I've enjoyed life to the fullest, even the not so good times.

This is just another entry in my journal…

Happy Birthday to my grandchild JaMir!

Get well JayDa, your mother loves you so much!

Love Sharon Wheeler

Reading the entry in my grandmother's notebook dating back to the day I entered this world, really had me emotional. Tears continuously fell down my face; I missed my grandmother so much. My grandmother was such a supportive person and a strong woman. One thing my grandmother taught me about being a male and expressing emotions was that I'm human so regardless if I'm male or not, there was nothing wrong with me expressing my feelings or showing an emotional side to or with others. Many males that I grew up with, attended school with, and even played basketball with, were also raised in single parent homes by a female (primarily their mothers or grandmothers). They were also taught that there was nothing wrong with crying, hugging, and simply expressing their feelings to others. I've been around other males including some family members who felt as though it made them less of a man when or if they cried, hugged another man, and did or said anything that involved them expressing their feelings to others. My father grew up with a male leader in the home but didn't really express his feelings much, with the exception of him doing so to and with my mother before I was born. I found out that many males who grew up with only a female parental figure, seemed to express their feelings more openly with and to others. I don't plan on having children anytime soon but when that time comes I will show this letter to my child when they're old enough to understand it:

My Unborn Child

Life is full of surprises many are good surprises and many are bad ones but you have to make choices that impact your life in either positive or negative ways. I will do whatever it takes to remain in your life, raise you right, and love you unconditionally. You just make sure you' re doing what it takes to treat others right, carry yourself accordingly, and love God as He loved and will love you! I learned a lot in my past from the mistakes I made and the mistakes that others made that were around and close to me. Never be afraid to come to me about anything, I will listen to your worries, concerns, and cries and love you with an open mind, heart, and soul. Your paternal grandmother died long before you were born and I don' t remember her because she died when I was just a few days old, but your paternal great-grandmother kept her memory alive by talking to me daily about her, and also keeping her items and showing them to me! Feel free to make your own decisions just be sure to try your best to let them be positive ones that will not hurt you or anyone else. Keep God first, others next, then yourself – all with good and loving intentions!

Signed this 20th day of September 1998

Love Dad (JaMir A. Wheeler)

I went through my personal belongings of letters, journals, and other writings a little while longer that Sunday night and read this in which my mother had written, shortly before my arrival into this world:

My Love

I've carried you months and
the time is approaching
For you to come through the forefront and give the world
more than simple hoping

I'm a little down right now

but no matter what happens today Remember that the

sorrows right now

Should never prevent you from kneeling to pray

You're a blessing from above Growing

inside of me and preparing To take on the

many journeys of love That are ahead of you

and waiting For you to work hard and

diligently

Towards the wonderful opportunities in life That not only you, but me, we

Us and the entire world need to grasp so tight Love Mom

(Wednesday July 22, 1998)

Today is Saturday October 31, 1998 and I'm standing in the midst of so much joy! I graduated from Basic Training earlier today and so many wonderful people came to witness it. I woke up this morning and was happy just to be willing and able to be one step closer to another milestone in my success! Before I knew it I was dressed in my military uniform and sitting on my bunk, waiting to line up for the ceremony. I graduated from Basic Training and was an official member of the United States Military, in the Navy Service Branch! All of the hard work and dedication I put in over the past nine weeks or so, had paid off and much more success was ahead of me. Pastor and First Lady Brown, Tianna, Tianna's brother Tre' and their parents, Kemari, Monah, Kamara, my Grandma and Grandpa Lewis, Mr. Mitchell, and some of the church members from back home all traveled from Queens New York all the way to Fort Worth Texas, to witness me graduate from Basic Training!

I was a very happy young man today and still am! At the young age of eighteen I've accomplished more than I've ever thought I would! My mother, grandmother, and father weren't in attendance, but they were with me in spirit and in my heart. I was thinking about all of them so much on my special day.

I'm ready and willing to take on whatever other opportunities lay ahead of me in this world and in my life!

Going to feed my face and enjoy my time with my family and friends!

JaMir Signing Out.....

(4:30 p.m.)

5. "Retracing Steps"

Now that I'm an adult, I often look back over my life and evaluate many situations. I've been told so many times over the years to "Live Life With No Regrets" but although I have no regrets, I always wished things in life would've happened differently. My mother lived a very short life and I never got to know her, so I wish the hands of time could change by her still being alive. Being upset at my father for him not being there for my mother during her time of need is and could've been a natural feeling of emotion, but what would it change? I'm not the only person in this world who has gone or will go through painful situations. My grandmother lived with cancer flowing through her body and didn't tell anyone she had cancer, raised a young man, lost her daughter, but through it all she never gave up... My best friend Kemari Harper was separated from his siblings off and on for a while until him and his twin sister Kamara were united together again, but he never gave up... These are just two examples of people in my life who didn't give up on others or themselves, so I will not ever give up on myself and neither should anyone else!

When people go after goals, many of them lack the ability to successfully or completely achieve their goals. I'm far from perfect; I've made numerous mistakes, still make mistakes, and will make many more mistakes until the day I leave this world. I steered away from a huge goal I planned to go after with three important people in my life, but sometimes in life our goals have to be steered in different directions. After

Basic Training, I did a lot of thinking about some roads I traveled on in my life. I didn't regret the fact that I decided to go into the military, but I still couldn't accept the fact that I left one of my largest dreams of helping young people. True indeed I owned a business involving the care of children and youth, but I had not physically been there to contribute to the organization. I had to do something but I didn't know exactly what that "something" was... I knew I could always turn to something in particular, so I PRAYED!

I thought hard, slept hard, and prayed hard about my feelings regarding my Childcare Center, me being in the military, and so much more. I had been talking to the Military Personnel about what my next steps following Basic Training would be. Things had really started to look up for me because not even two days following my Basic Training Graduation, I received a call from a Naval Base in New York City, New York. I went back to Queens with my family, friends, and church family following graduation. I was at home that Monday morning when I received the call and I was so excited to get an offer in the area. The personnel on the Naval Base wanted me to come in for an interview the following morning, so we could all meet and discuss the protocol. I was the only person residing in my grandmother's house (which was left to me following her passing a few years back) besides when it was time for the youth, Kemari, Kamara, and Monah to be in the house for the Children's Center Afterschool Program. That Monday afternoon I was so overwhelmed with love because I finally saw my youth for the first time since I was back and witnessed the wonderful establishment of the "S & J Wheeler Children's Center." Besides Kamara, Monah, and Kemari, Tre' was the first to greet me when he walked in the door that afternoon. I was so excited to be home doing what I loved and that was helping the youth! The Center closed for the day that evening and after closing time, my three co-founders and I all cleaned up. I talked to them letting them know I had a lot on my mind pertaining to my goals but God answered my prayers that previous night. Even though I wanted to be in the military I felt isolated and back tracked in my admirations because I didn't go through with my goal of opening up and running the Children's Center. My friends were so supportive and had always been; they let me know whatever I needed to do to fulfill my personal goals and desires in life, then I needed to do so. The three of them were in college in Queens, rotating shifts at the Center, cheering, and playing basketball for the school. They all let me know that they were satisfied with how their lives were maintaining and progressing but wanted me to be content with my life and goals. I let them know that I had a meeting with the Military Personnel in New York City the next morning and hopefully, I would be stationed there because I wasn't comfortable relocating somewhere too far away from home. I was still only eighteen years of age and even though I was legally an adult, I was still very young so I had a lot more growing to do. Kamara, Monah, and Kemari all left after we talked and then I called Tianna on the telephone. I let her know that I wanted to talk to her so I asked her would she like to come to my house or would she like for us to meet somewhere. Tianna let me know that she could come to my house, so I waited for her to arrive...

Fifteen minutes, thirty minutes, an hour, then two hours passed by and Tianna still hadn't arrived at my house. I had begun to worry because she and I didn't live far from one another at all, so I wanted to know why it was taking her so long to get to my house. I finally decided to call Tianna back at home and when I did, Tre' answered the phone. I spoke on the phone to my little buddy and asked him did Tianna leave their house yet. He told me that she was home with her friend; I immediately asked him to speak to her. Tre' went to get her and a few minutes later, she got on the phone. I was worried that something happened to her on the way to my house but when I found out she was home with her friend, I became disappointed. Tianna got on the phone not knowing who was on the other end because Tre' didn't tell her who was on the phone. I asked Tianna did she forget to come to my house and there was about a five second period of silence then she replied, "I totally forgot." I let Tianna know that I really needed to talk to her about some things but she just abandoned me. She was really quiet and wouldn't say much, she didn't even apologize. Something had to be going on with her; she was distancing herself from me, we hadn't seen one another all weekend, and I was very concerned. I couldn't stay on the phone with Tianna any longer so I ended the conversation short and told her I would talk to her later. I immediately gathered my wallet, keys, jacket, and headed out the door. I wasn't in a good mood and I needed to release some bad energy, so I decided to walk to Tianna's house instead of driving a few blocks because I indeed needed to figure out what was going on with her.

I arrived at Tianna's house fifteen minutes after I departed my house and when I walked up to the porch, she was sitting on the stoop with a guy. The guy that was sitting on the porch with her went to high school with me and we played on the school basketball team together. Everyone's entitled to have friends but the two of them seemed to be more than just friends. Tianna and the guy whose name was Justin, were hugged up with one another on the porch. I've never been a mean person so I tried to keep my cool and not let my emotions get the worse of me when I saw the two of them hugged up together. All I could think about was the fact that she had been an important part of my life for some time and I wanted to talk to her about being stationed closer to home, as well as us taking our relationship towards the direction of marriage. I was speechless when I saw the two of them on the porch together and was angry but I didn't want to do or say anything that I would end up regretting, so I just turned around and left. Tianna ran after me calling my name until she caught up with me. She apologized to me and said she and Justin started hanging out and then they started to get closer. I really didn't say much, I was just really in need of her understanding regarding my feelings of loneliness and betrayal. Justin and I weren't friends but we weren't enemies either. I let Tianna know that I put my all out for and to her but she obviously didn't feel the same about me. I thought what we had was real but it obviously wasn't. I walked off and couldn't listen to her at that time; so much was running through my mind and heart.

That night I evaluated so much and even though I worked hard, completed high school, entered the military, had a house and a car, and plenty of money saved up... I still wasn't at a happy place within myself. Anybody can have all of the money in the world, but still not be happy. I lost my mother, grandmother, father for some time, and now I lost the girl I thought would be by my side for the rest of our lives. My father was thousands of miles away and was searching for peace within himself, so I didn't feel as though I could go to him for comfort. I knew I could pray and I could do that in the comfort of my own home as I often did. An eighteen year old male who has lost important relationships in his life, really was in desperate need of some uplifting. I had to go to New York City in the morning but wasn't at peace with myself that night so I decided to go to Pastor and First Lady Brown's house. I didn't call them because I really needed some face-to-face advice and I also knew that they would accept me with open arms, and would never turn me away.

When I got to the Brown's home, I rang the doorbell and First Lady Brown answered the door. She obviously noticed I wasn't feeling alright so she immediately walked up to me and hugged me. After about a minute or two of embracing one another, we both walked inside. Whenever First Lady Brown wants to hold long conversations, she does them in her kitchen while drinking coffee. First Lady Brown offered me some coffee but I didn't really drink coffee, so I took some lemonade. She told me she made some baked spaghetti, garlic bread, and salad for dinner earlier and offered me some. I rarely ever turned food down and even though I wasn't in the best mood, I still didn't turn it down at that moment either. We both sat at the table eating, drinking coffee and lemonade, and talking. I really opened up to her about how so much had been going on in my life. I never really gave myself time to cope, heal, adjust, and adapt to the numerous changes that had entered my path in life. Life comes with changes but I was so young to have so much happen to me, especially losses. We talked for about an hour and I let her know so much within that time frame regarding my family, career in the military, and the recent separation of Tianna and I. First Lady Brown let me know that I didn't give myself any "JaMir Time" because I gave so much of myself to others: I dedicated myself to the military at a young age, opened up a business in my home at a young age, and even tried to commit spending the rest of my life with someone else at a young age. I had to step back and look things over so I could realize where I needed to be mentally. In a way I think

I rebelled from myself by not loving ME after I lost out on so much in my life. Yes I had many people tell me they loved me, cared for me, and so much more but the only person besides God that I can truly depend on to love me is JaMir Antonio Wheeler. I really enjoyed the one-on-one talk I had with her and I thanked her for listening and talking to me. I headed home that night and felt a large burden lifted off of my shoulders. I knew I needed to make some necessary changes in my life and I was going to take some steps to change them.

The next morning I prepared myself to go to the Naval Base in New York City. When I arrived in New York City, I was in love with the atmosphere; it was congested like Queens but it was so nice looking. The meeting started promptly at 9:00 a.m. and lasted about forty-five minutes. Personnel explained the details of what I would be required to do on the base and that I would be working four days for twelve hours then be off for three days. This particular base was one of the many main bases in which training relating with communication and computer specialists, finance, cooks, administrative, and many other careers were held. I was told that at any given moment I could be deployed on ships or submarines and after I was told that, I really thought about the fact that I would be away from home again like I was when I went to Texas for Training. I had to report back to the base the very next morning to begin training as a Computer Specialist. I had been trained in Basic Training when I was in Texas but this was going to be the start of something more long term for me, and I was at peace with it.

I called my father later that afternoon to talk to him and besides, I hadn't talked to him in a few days. I let Kenny know that I had been thinking about a lot over the past few days and after the one-on-one important talk with First Lady Brown about myself, I decided to close the Children's Center. My father listened to me without judging my decisions or disagreeing with my opinions. I let him know that for so many years I had been trying to do things to please others, but now it was time for me to step back and really put myself on the path I wanted to be on. I wanted to come back to Jamaica Queens so bad but for what? I thought so much was waiting for me but even though I had important people there, I still had to find myself and do something with my life that would leave a great impact. I still needed time to grow; I wasn't mentally or emotionally ready to run a business. My father and I had a nice little conversation and it felt good to get some things off of my chest. He was still doing well on his job, had a little apartment to himself, had been reporting to his parole officer on time for every meeting, and was present when they stopped by on his job or at his apartment.

A meeting was scheduled at the center involving Kemari, Monah, Kamara, and I. I called the meeting to discuss my plans of closing the center. All three of them were confused as to why I decided to shut the center down so I fully went into detail regarding how my life just didn't seem to be in a good place. I let them know that I backtracked and I needed to edit some things in my life. I had been writing things down relating with my feelings, just following in my grandmother and mother's footsteps, but I didn't think that was really something I wanted to do. Just because we admire, care, and love others, doesn't mean we have to follow their dreams in hopes of accomplishing ours. Who knew where I would be and what I would be doing in the future but I knew if I wasn't happy with myself in my present, I couldn't move forward towards progression in my future. Kemari stood up in our meeting and expressed to me that he totally understood where I was coming from, and that he wanted me to do whatever I needed to do in order to be at a better place with myself. I really needed to hear the words that Kemari spoke to me because they were words from someone else who was the same age as me, and I thanked him for empathizing with me. Shortly after the three of them left, I received a call from personnel at the Naval Base in New York City in which I had recently met with...

Something had occurred which I anticipated would, but I didn't expect it would happen that soon. I thought back to the day I was sworn into the military; I didn't think I would embark on such a large role of pathways in my life but I wouldn't complain, because I think it was destined for me. What wasn't destined for me was me adapting to and with the rhythm of others, I had to create my own rhythm. I was informed that I would be deployed to Japan in a few weeks. I would leave from the Naval Station in Norfolk Virginia, then head to Japan from there. I had just a couple of weeks to let all of the youth from the Children's Center, their parents, and other responsible parties involved know that the center would soon be closing for business. Numerous people were saddened by the news but one person in particular was very saddened by the news and that was Tre'. Tre' didn't like the idea of the "S & J Wheeler Children's Center" closing and he expressed to me that he was very upset. I talked to him for a while just him and I, letting him know that changes are a part of life and sometimes our positive changes make others upset, but they help us. I explained to him that I had to go on another path of success in my life but I wasn't doing it to hurt him or anyone else, I was doing it to help myself. I spent a lot of time with the youth over the next few days, enjoying time with all of them before the center closed.

The "S & J Wheeler Children's Center" officially closed for operation on a Friday and although it made me sad watching the children leave and I knew they wouldn't be returning, I was at peace with it. That weekend my father surprised me by coming to town; he was allowed to come spend the weekend in Queens New York before I left for deployment for three years. My father stayed at my house with me from that Friday night up until that Sunday night; we played basketball together, went to church together at my Grandmother and Grandfather Lewis' church, cleaned up the remainder of the things I had left to clean in the Children's Center, spent a little time with the Lewis family, and so much more within those three days and two nights. I only had about ten days left until I would be heading out for deployment. I didn't have much left to do besides prepare for my departure mentally, emotionally, and physically. My house would be vacant; Pastor and First Lady Lewis, my paternal grandparents, and my three best friends promised to always check on my house. I decided to leave my car at the Naval Base in a storage building; personnel would check on my car and keep it in good shape.

After my father left to go back to South Carolina, I decided to relax at home in front of the television. That night around 9:00 the doorbell rang. I looked out of the peep hole and Tianna was standing on the porch, and looked as if she had been crying. I opened the door and invited her in; we might have recently gone through a separation but I still loved her and was concerned about her well-being. We sat at the table in the kitchen and talked about what was on her mind. She really poured her all out to me that night about how she knew she made a huge mistake leaving me, she wasn't doing too well in school, and Justin wasn't the guy she thought he was. I listened to her open up to me and I did it without judging her mistakes neither did I throw her wrong doing towards me, in her face. Listening is a silent action in which I learned to do in Mr. Mitchell's English Class in high school. Tianna needed someone to talk to and listen to her so she depended on me for that need, so I didn't want to let her down no matter what I was going through. I let her know when people aren't happy, they need to figure out where they need to be mentally, in order to be happy. She wasn't happy with Justin but I told her it wasn't my place to make calls regarding their relationship, so she needed to realize what she needed to do for herself. We finished talking about what was on her mind then we relaxed; we watched television and reminisced about the good times we shared together. Tianna let me know that she regretted the fact that she treated me so poorly when all I had been was a good man to her. I forgave her and reminded her that everybody makes mistakes. She didn't know about my deployment so that night I let her know I would be leaving soon and even though we weren't together, she still had a place in my heart. I let her know I would take her home so she wouldn't walk home alone in the dark. Instead of me driving Tianna a few blocks to her house we walked and talked some more, in the process. I spoke to her parents before I left their home from dropping her off and told them to take care, giving them my farewell (Tre' was in bed asleep so I didn't get to talk to him). My walk home was peaceful and I took my time walking back home from Tianna's house.

The next few days I would spend in the states, would be reflection time; reality really was setting in about me leaving the country for a few years. I did many things by myself during the last days I was in Queens. I went down to the court like Kemari and I started to do when we were younger and continued to do throughout our teenage years, but I was alone this time. One afternoon I walked to the court and just shot my basketball around. While I was shooting around I thought I heard a familiar voice so I turned around and there was Tre', with a few older guys. I thought the guys looked familiar as I thought about where I knew them from and it hit me... Those guys went to high school with me. Something seemed strange: Why would a junior high school teenager be with some guys who had already graduated from high school? I didn't want to assume things because those guys could've been positive role models to Tre' but something just didn't seem right about it. I continued to shoot around but at the same time, I was starting to look around a lot to be more aware of my surroundings. After shooting around for a little while longer, I heard some loud gun shots along with someone yelling.

I grabbed my ball and began to quickly leave the court but all of a sudden, someone was repeatedly yelling my name for help. I tried to figure out what direction the yelling was coming from, because I already knew whose voice it was and it was none other than the voice of Tre'. I then dropped my ball so I could locate Tre' and figure out what was happening. As I was running through the same walkway in which Kemari, Monah, and I hid in one time when we were younger when gunshots erupted, I stumbled over someone. At that very moment I was terrified because there was Tre' laying in a pool of blood, in that very same walkway. Tre' was responsive but was in a lot of pain. I refused to ask him what happened because I could clearly see that he had been shot,

I just didn't know exactly where Tre' had been shot at on his body. Someone was running past us where I stumbled over Tre' so I yelled for them to get some help fast, because someone had been shot. Not too long after I yelled for help, the paramedics and police arrived. Tre' was checked out at the scene and taken to a nearby Queens' area hospital; I rode with Tre' in the ambulance because I refused to leave him alone. I had never been in an ambulance and never wanted to be in one but I saw that Tre' was in pain and for him to be as young as he was and had been shot, all of that was too much for him.

We arrived at the hospital about ten minutes later and Tre' had been stripped of his clothes by the paramedics, so they could better tend to his wounds. He also had to be hooked up to oxygen due to his major loss of blood and his breathing complications. The paramedics let me know that they would turn Tre' over to the doctors and asked me to sit in the waiting area, and to also call his family. I was confused and scared for young Tre' but I held it together for him. I immediately called Tre' and Tianna's house to let their parents know he had been shot and they needed to come to the hospital. Tre's parents and his sister Tianna, all arrived at the hospital ten minutes after I called them. All of us sat in the waiting area worried about Tre' while we were waiting on the doctors to let us know something about his condition. Every fifteen to twenty minutes, each of us would take turns and go to the Check-In desk in the lobby, to see if we could get any kind of update on Tre'. Every time one of us went to the desk to inquire about his condition, they would let us know that the doctors were still tending to him and they would let us know something as soon as the doctors did.

After two hours of sitting in the Waiting Area, a male doctor fully clothed in scrubs approached all of us. The doctor informed us that they needed to talk to us. He let us know that Tre' lost a significant amount of blood as a result of his two gunshot wounds to his back and one gunshot wound to his left hip. Tianna's mother had been crying the whole time so their father was comforting her, making sure she was ok. Tianna had been crying but had stopped; I comforted her in the Waiting Area. The doctor then informed us that we would need to come with him to a private room so he could explain to us in detail, the severity of Tre's condition. He asked for only the immediate family to go with him and I was going to stay in the Waiting Area until Tianna and Tre's father let the doctor know I was family, and was coming back with them as well. We all sat around a table in the private room we went to and he started to explain to us that a bullet had entered Tre's back piercing his spine, and they were unable to remove the bullet. The doctor had some x-ray photos of his spine with the bullet lodged in his spine and it was very noticeable that he endured major pain. Thankfully they were able to remove two of the three bullets but they were unsuccessful with removing the third one. Tre' was paralyzed from the neck down and when we got that devastating news, we all broke down crying. We had to be strong and pull ourselves together because we were about to go in the room in which Tre' was stationed, to visit with him.

Before we went into the room where Tre' was located, I had some thoughts racing through my head. I thought back to the incident in which my father was involved in relating with him shooting and killing someone, then spending eighteen years in prison. I didn't understand how a child so young, would be in the hospital paralyzed from gunshot wounds. Some things in life just happen and we just don't know or might not ever know why, but I couldn't ponder on that for long, I had to go in and visit with my buddy Tre'. The four of us got ourselves together and helped calm one another down, and then we headed into the room in which Tre' was located.

Tre's father and step-mother entered the room first and Tianna and I were closely behind them. Tre' had been propped up in the hospital bed so he could see us. He had been sleep prior to us entering his room but was awake when we arrived in the room. Tre' didn't have an oxygen mask hooked up to his face anymore but he looked very uncomfortable. Tre' and Tianna's father began to talk to Tre' and told him not to worry about anything because they were there for him. Tre' began to cry and express his anger towards himself. Tre' continued to talk and let his father know he didn't understand why he couldn't move any of his body parts. Tianna told him to calm down and not upset himself. It took a little while for him to calm down and before we knew it, a detective had knocked on the door and entered the room. The detective let Tre's father and step-mother know he was there to get some information from Tre', relating with the shooting which caused his injury. He let us know we didn't have to leave the room because we were family and more importantly, he was a minor so his parents needed to stay in the room during questioning. The detective stayed for about twenty-five minutes and the responses Tre' had provided to the detective, shocked us all.

Earlier that day before the shooting incident involving Tre', he walked to the court with Justin to play basketball. The two of them shot the ball around for a while then a few guys walked up and began to talk to Justin. While Justin was talking to the guys that walked up, Tre' continued to shoot the ball around on the court. Justin walked away with them for a while then went back to the court with Tre' and told him he had to go home, but would be back. Justin explained to Tre' that he had to hang out with those guys he was talking to until he got back, but he couldn't explain to him why. Tre' let the detective know that one of the guys had a gun and when he tried to follow Justin, they stepped in front of him and told him he had to stay with them until Justin returned to the court. Tre' sat on the bleachers at the court with the guys for about an hour. Tre' and the guys were getting upset because Justin was taking too long to return and somewhere in between that time, I walked up to the court but didn't realize Tre' was in any kind of trouble. I immediately began to feel guilty when I heard him explain in detail what happened; I could've done something to help him but I didn't. Tre' continued to explain the incident to the detective and it was apparent that Justin was in trouble. While I was shooting my ball around at the court, Justin returned. All of a sudden shots broke out and people started to scatter. In the midst of everyone running in different directions, Tre' was hit by a few bullets. Justin didn't just go back to the court, he brought a gun with him. Justin yelled to Tre' that he needed to run and then shortly afterwards, gunfire exchanged between Justin and one of the other guys who also had a gun.

I really felt horrible because Tre' was in need of help and I didn't help him. Tianna began to cry then stormed out of the room. I followed her and tried to calm her down but she was too upset. She wasn't upset with me like I thought she was, she was upset with Justin and the fact that he put her little brother in harm's way. I then let Tianna know that I could've helped Tre' but I didn't realize he was in trouble until it was too late. She stopped crying and asked me why didn't I tell her I was at the court during the time Tre' had been shot. I let her know everything happened so fast and I stayed with him from the time he was shot up until the time he arrived at the hospital on the ambulance. She apologized to me and told me it wasn't my fault but she stressed her eagerness to figure out why Justin would put her brother in danger like he did. We talked for a little while longer then went back in Tre's room.

The detective let their parents know he would continue to investigate and would also send authorities out to arrest Justin and the other guys, which were involved in the shooting. I had a few days left in Queens and I felt bad about leaving. Many things happen in life and I can't fix all of them; if I could fix a lot of things I'd have my mother and grandmother back in my life. I hung out with Tre' at the hospital for a while and let him know I would soon be leaving town for deployment. I assured him he would be alright and even though he couldn't walk or move most of his body, he would be well taken care of.

Justin and the other three guys who were involved in the shooting incident were apprehended later that day and taken into custody. The fate of their future would be left up to the legal system and other responsible parties when the time approached. I didn't write any letters, didn't want a Going Away Party or Get Together, or anything else special for my departure, I just told everyone that it was time for me to go on a new journey in my life, in peace. I spent some time with family and friends but I mostly spent some well-needed time with myself. Wherever I go in life, I want to assure myself that I will be happy and content about the paths I choose to walk on. Moving on to other missions was what I was embarking on and I refused to look back with regrets, pain, and anything else that would hinder me from progression and success.

Retracing Steps

My pathways in life might have been and maybe will be uneven, but the pathways in my life are specifically for me. I left Jamaica Queens New York in November of 1998 for deployment to Japan as a more humble, aware, and blessed young man...

ABOUT THE AUTHOR

CHENELLE MONIQUE WILES was born in Washington D.C. and lived in Landover Maryland with her family until she moved to Charlotte N.C. when she was a young child, and was raised there throughout the remainder of her youthful years. She has dedicated a lot of her time to working with youth, leads Youth Motivational Speeches and Workshops, is a Youth and Young Adult Mentor, and enjoys writing books pertaining to children and the younger generation. Her first book I'M NOT A CELEBRITY BUT I HAVE A STORY was released in December of 2011; an autobiography containing personal struggles she endured in her childhood years in which she overcame. She stepped up to help the youth so they wouldn't give up when difficult situations entered their lives. This fictional novel is a representation of how youth can utilize the help that is given to them in this world, but ultimately step up by independently making successful decisions which will impact their lives....